"Taste the pie. It's guaranteed to make you smile."

Erik did as he was told. Stupid as it was, he liked having her nearby, tempting him to take a mouthful of the forbidden fruit. À la mode was an added bonus.

Sure enough, it made him smile. "You win."

"I always do. You know what would be great? For us to go out and play together. There's a gallery opening tomorrow night that I really want to see. You can take me to it, if you're free."

He looked at her as if she'd flipped her lovely little lid. Her suggestion sounded suspiciously like a date. "You don't need an older guy like me taking you anywhere."

"You're not old. You're yummy."

Yummy? His heart beat hard in his chest. *Bang. Bang. Bang.* Like shots from a gun. His daughter wanted him to start dating again. But he doubted that she had someone like Dana in mind.

"Say yes, Eric."

* * *

FAMILY RENEWAL:
Sometimes all it takes is a second chance

Dear Reader,

Have you ever wondered how books are titled? Who comes up with the name and how it's decided upon? Mostly it's up to the author to make suggestions, then it goes to editorial, where they either chose a title from the list the author submitted or make new suggestions, based on the marketing of the book.

Thinking up titles has always been a challenge for me. I never seem to have just the right one floating around in my head. I appreciate that it's not solely up to me. Some of my favorite titles were created by editors or marketing executives.

But I have to say, *Lost and Found Husband* came naturally to me for this book. I titled the first book in my Family Renewal duet *Lost and Found Father* because the hero in that story had given up his baby daughter for adoption and was being reunited with her eighteen years later. In this book, the hero (who is that child's adoptive parent) was once a happy and well-adjusted husband who'd tragically lost his wife. Now he is in a position to be a husband all over again, to start fresh, to regain the joy that he'd lost, only with someone new.

So...I give you *Lost and Found Husband,* a book with an emotionally wounded hero and the lovely young woman who helps him find his way back home.

Hugs and Happily Ever After,

Sheri WhiteFeather

Lost and Found Husband

—

Sheri WhiteFeather

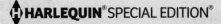 HARLEQUIN® SPECIAL EDITION®

Recycling programs
for this product may
not exist in your area.

ISBN-13: 978-0-373-65774-2

LOST AND FOUND HUSBAND

Copyright © 2013 by Sheree Henry-Whitefeather

Printed in U.S.A.

Books by Sheri WhiteFeather

Harlequin Special Edition

ΔThe Texan's Future Bride #2255
+Lost and Found Father #2284
+Lost and Found Husband #2292

Silhouette Romantic Suspense

Mob Mistress #1469
Killer Passion #1520
*Imminent Affair #1586
*Protecting Their Baby #1590

Silhouette Bombshell

Always Look Twice #27
Never Look Back #84

Silhouette Desire

Warrior's Baby #1248
Skyler Hawk: Lone Brave #1272
Jesse Hawk: Brave Father #1278
Cheyenne Dad #1300
Night Wind's Woman #1332
Tycoon Warrior #1364
Cherokee #1376

Comanche Vow #1388
Cherokee Marriage Dare #1478
Sleeping with Her Rival #1496
Cherokee Baby #1509
Cherokee Dad #1523
The Heart of a Stranger #1527
Cherokee Stranger #1563
A Kept Woman #1575
Steamy Savannah Nights #1597
Betrayed Birthright #1663
Apache Nights #1678
Expecting Thunder's
   Baby #1742
Marriage of Revenge #1751
The Morning-After
   Proposal #1756

ΔByrds of a Feather
*Warrior Society
+Family Renewal

Other titles by this author
available in ebook format.

SHERI WHITEFEATHER

is a bestselling author who has won numerous awards, including readers' and reviewers' choice honors. She writes a variety of romance novels for Harlequin. She has become known for incorporating Native American elements into her stories. She has two grown children who are tribally enrolled members of the Muscogee Creek Nation.

Sheri is of Italian-American descent. Her great-grandparents immigrated to the United States from Italy through Ellis Island, originating from Castel di Sangro and Sicily. She lives in California and enjoys ethnic dining, shopping in vintage stores and going to art galleries and museums. Sheri loves to hear from her readers. Visit her website at www.SheriWhiteFeather.com.

Chapter One

Eric Reeves was dining in an eatery near his Southern California home, watching Dana Peterson, the bubbly blonde waitress, bring food to another table. His dinner, meat loaf and mashed potatoes, was only half-eaten.

He kept his gaze trained on Dana. With her bold pink uniform and her nicely curved figure, she was a sight to behold. They weren't friends, per se, but they'd built a friendly rapport through snippets of server-customer conversation. Eric ate here often.

When his wife was alive, he used to eat at home. Back then, everything had been wonderfully normal. But he'd lost Corrine seven years ago, and it had become a long and lonely road since then.

Dana whizzed past him on her way to the kitchen and smiled, her ponytail swishing. She was a twenty-six-year-old working her way through community college and enjoying the wherever-it-took-her experience. Eric was forty-two with a grounded job and a grown daughter. He and Dana didn't have much in common, except that his daughter was a college student, too.

By the time he finished his meal, Dana returned to his table. She shot him another of her upbeat smiles. Today she was wearing a purple iris fastened behind her ear. She always wore a flower of some sort. Sometimes they were artificial flowers in trendy hair clips, like the aforementioned iris, and sometimes they were real.

A while back, she'd given him one of the real McCoys when he'd revealed that he was widowed. She had always pegged him for divorced, and to make up for her error, she'd removed the flower she wore that day, a velvety red rose, and placed it gently in his hand. Later, he'd gone to Corrine's grave and left it for her. Somewhere along the way, he'd gotten used to talking to his dead wife. He'd even explained where the rose had come from, telling her about the warm-hearted waitress who'd bestowed it upon him.

"Can I get you anything else?" Dana asked.

He shook his head.

"You sure? The apple pie is fresh."

He thought she was fresh, too, light and springy—a modern bohemian, as she called herself, who'd yet to decide on a college major.

"Cherry is my favorite," he said.

"We don't have any cherry. But I promise the apple is delish."

He met her gaze. She had the bluest eyes and the blondest, most naturally golden hair. Everything about her shimmered.

She cocked her head. "What do you say? A la mode?"

He shifted his focus. Pie and ice cream. "Sure, okay."

"Coffee, too?"

"Yes."

Off she went: pink uniform, purple flower and Gidget ponytail. Eric found himself watching her again. He enjoyed looking at her. He enjoyed it far too much.

He was frowning when she delivered his coffee and dessert.

"What's wrong?" she asked.

You, he thought. He didn't want to be attracted to a woman who was closer to his daughter's age than his own.

"Nothing is wrong."

"Taste the pie." She waggled her fingers. "It's guaranteed to make you smile."

He did as he was told. Stupid as it was, he liked having her nearby, tempting him to take a mouthful of the forbidden fruit. The a la mode was an added bonus.

Sure enough, it made him smile. "You win."

"I always do. You know what would be great? There's a gallery opening tomorrow night that I really want to see. You can take me to it, if you're free."

He looked at her as if she'd flipped her lovely little lid. Her suggestion sounded suspiciously like a date. "You don't need an older guy like me taking you anywhere."

"You're not old. You're barely into your forties. Besides, you're yummy."

Yummy? His heart hit his chest. *Bang. Bang. Bang.* Like shots from a gun. His daughter wanted him to start dating again. But he doubted that she had someone like Dana in mind.

"Say yes, Eric."

He didn't utter a word. Instead he took a second bite, but the diversion didn't work. The gooey sweetness made him want to tug her onto his lap and kiss her hard and fast. To curb his appetite, he swigged his coffee.

She persisted. "Come on. It'll be fun. Besides, you're an artist. You'll be the perfect companion for a gallery opening."

He downplayed his profession. "I'm an art teacher at a middle school."

"You're still an artist. How about this? I'll give you my number, and you can call and let me know."

She zoomed off to tend to other customers, and he ate the devil out of his pie.

A short while later she returned with his check and her number, written on a scrap of paper. Eric tucked it into his pocket. He had no idea what he was going to do, but at least he had a day to think about it.

"I hope I see you tomorrow," she said, placing her hand on his shoulder.

He wished that she hadn't touched him. The kiss he'd longed for came tumbling back. "I just don't know." He gazed at her mouth.

She moistened her lips. "You'll figure it out."

Would he? She was the first woman he'd desired since Corrine had died. He didn't know what that said about his libido, considering Dana's carefree attitude and age. "I've been out of the loop since my wife passed."

"Ours will be just a casual date."

"That doesn't change the age difference between us."

"It isn't that big of a difference."

It was to him. Even as attracted as he was to Dana,

he'd never considered dating a twentysomething. "I'll call you and let you know either way."

"Okay. Thanks. I better get back to work now." She touched his shoulder again, rubbing it a little this time.

His stomach flip-flopped.

After she was gone, he paid with cash and left her a generous tip. On his way to the door, he turned around and looked for her, seeking her attention from across the diner.

She caught his gaze and flashed a don't-forget-to-call-me smile.

As if forgetting about her was actually possible.

After work Dana went home, excited about the possibility of going out with Eric. Even if he chose not to date her, she would still be proud of herself for putting it out there. She'd had a crush on him since she'd first met him, which was when she'd started working at the diner, almost a year ago. A year was a record for her. Not just to hold a crush for that long, but to stay at the same job. She liked to mix things up.

And boy had she done that today. She'd finally mustered the courage to ask Eric out. She'd been thinking about it for what seemed like forever and now that Valentine's Day was around the corner, she figured this was the time to do it. Plus, when she'd heard about the gallery opening, she knew she'd found the perfect event to invite him to attend with her.

He was such an intriguing mystery, a man she wanted to get to know. She especially liked to see him smile. He had a great smile that he didn't use nearly often enough.

She went into her bedroom to change. She lived

in the most adorable guest house that she'd found on Craigslist. Her side of the yard, which had a white picket fence, hosted an English-style garden and a naked-cherub fountain. The cherub amused her because he was one of those mischievous little angels that appeared to be peeing in the water. Everything about the place was perfect. She even had an awesome landlord who owned the property and lived in the front house. In fact, she and Candy McCall were becoming the best of friends. Prior to living here, Dana had been in an apartment crowded with roommates.

She tossed her uniform on a chair and climbed into a ragged T-shirt and comfy jeans. She was anxious to talk to Candy about Eric.

Dana ventured outside. The weather was lovely on this February evening. As she passed the cherub, she smiled.

After crossing her flower-filled yard, she entered through the gate that led to Candy's equally colorful residence.

She approached the back door and called out through the screen. "Hey, you! Can I pop in for a minute? I have some news."

"Of course" was the reply. "Get your butt in here."

Dana happily entered. Candy was in her cluttered kitchen, preparing what most people would assume were regular cookies, but Dana knew they were home-made dog treats that had just come out of the oven. Candy was a yoga instructor who also taught classes in doga: yoga for dogs. On top of that, she was a strikingly beautiful, long-legged brunette who ate a strict vegetarian diet, burned luscious-smelling candles and spoke evasively about her failed marriage.

"Where's Yogi?" Dana asked, inquiring about Candy's yellow lab and the queen of doga.

"Napping. So what's your news?"

"I asked him to take me on a date."

"Him? Your hottie customer?"

Dana nodded. "I even told him that he was yummy." She relayed her conversation with Eric. "I'm going to plan my wardrobe for tomorrow night, just in case."

"Good idea. Send it into the universe and make it happen."

"The hippy-dippy way?"

"Yep."

They laughed. Hippy-dippy was a phrase Dana's mom used to describe her free-spirited lifestyle. Mom was much more conservative, aside from the wild one-nighter she'd had with Dana's elusive dad.

Candy turned serious. "When did Eric's wife pass away?"

"Seven years ago."

"And he hasn't dated since?"

"That's the impression I got. He said he's been out of the loop since then."

"Does he have any kids?"

"A daughter. She's a business major at UCLA, with a minor in women's studies."

"She sounds interesting. Have you ever met her?"

"No. He's never brought her to the diner. He's never even told me her name. But he speaks highly of her."

"What else do you know about him?"

"Besides him being a widowed art teacher with an eighteen-year-old daughter? Nothing, except that I want to go out with him and make him smile."

"This isn't a fixer-upper project, is it?"

"What do you mean?"

"He sounds a bit broken, and you're drawn to troubled people, Dana."

"You're not troubled." She amended her statement. "Well, maybe you are, but that's not why I'm friends with you."

Naturally, Candy didn't remark on her state of mind. They both knew that she'd yet to make peace with her divorce.

Instead she asked, "Did Eric ever tell you how his wife died?"

"She had cancer. But he never said what kind or how long her battle lasted. He only mentioned it briefly."

"How badly do you think he misses her?"

"I don't know, but I can tell that he's still struggling to get over her loss."

"Does that concern you?"

"Actually, I think it's nice that he loved her so much. What kind of man would he be if he'd never loved his wife?"

"Not a very good one," Candy replied, a tad too uncomfortably.

Dana studied her friend. Was that a reference to her ex? If it was, Candy wasn't saying anything else. And Dana didn't push her. Instead she said about Eric, "I really hope he agrees to go out with me."

"What happened to your plan-your-wardrobe-for-tomorrow-night confidence?"

"I guess I'm getting a little nervous that he'll decline the offer. But I'm still picking out something to wear. My crush on him isn't going away anytime soon."

Yogi came into the kitchen and yawned. Apparently she was up from her nap. Dana patted her head.

"Hey, sweetie." The dog wagged her tail and sniffed the canine-cookie air.

"Do you think Eric is a dog person or a cat person?" Candy asked.

"Hmm. Good question. I'd venture to guess cats." He had a catlike quality about him, warm but still somehow aloof. "You should see him. Tall and dark and chiseled. He's half Cherokee."

"How do you know what his heritage is?"

"He wore a Native Pride T-shirt once, and I asked him about it."

"So that's one more thing you know about him."

Dana nodded. "It isn't much, is it? For a whole year? But I haven't told him everything about myself, either. Mostly I just refill his water more than I should as an excuse to keep returning to his table."

"I'll bet he appreciates you doting on him."

"He certainly watches me a lot. I can always feel those dark eyes roving over me whenever I walk away."

"Sounds like a mutual crush."

"You have no idea how many times I've fantasized about him while I was in bed, moaning like a tart." For the sake of drama, she pulled a vintage Meg Ryan and demonstrated the noises she made.

Candy laughed. "Are you going to tell him that?"

She laughed, too. "Sure? Why not? I've been known to say what's on my mind." And these days Eric took up a lot of room in her mind. "I'm going to go dig through my closet now." She wanted to choose an ensemble that would please him. Maybe even something that showed off a bawdy bit of cleavage.

'Cause life was too important to waste.

* * *

Eric couldn't do it. He couldn't date someone as young as Dana. Hell, he couldn't date anyone at all. He wasn't ready, not even for something casual. Keeping to himself was easier.

He picked up his cell phone, intending to call Dana and decline her offer, but he dialed his daughter, Kaley, instead, needing to hear her voice.

She'd chosen to live in a dorm, even though her campus was fairly close to home. Eric supported her decision. He wanted his daughter to spread her wings, to find her independence, to enjoy her youth. But damn, he missed seeing her every day. Of course, she still came by on weekends sometimes. But between her studies and her social life, those weekend visits were becoming less frequent.

"Hi, Dad," she said, by way of a phone greeting.

"Hey, what are you doing?"

"Getting ready to go out. I'm going to a Valentine-themed party with my girlfriends. There's another one tomorrow night, too. Both of them are for singles only. How great is that?"

Valentine's Day was on Monday. It was a holiday he no longer celebrated, but apparently Kaley and her crowd were intent on enjoying it. He feigned an upbeat tone. "Sounds fun." It also sounded as if she wasn't going to be home any time this weekend.

"What are you doing?" she asked.

He almost said, "Nothing," but he didn't want her to feel bad for him, so he replied, "I was invited to a gallery opening tomorrow."

"Really? Are you going to go?"

"I don't know. I haven't decided." That was better than admitting the truth.

Kaley didn't ask who invited him. She probably thought it was one of his old artist friends. He wouldn't have told her who it was, anyway, so he was glad that she hadn't asked.

"You should see me, Dad. I'm wearing this cheesy pink gown." She laughed. "And a tiara. The party tonight is dress-up."

He smiled. She used to love wearing princess getups when she was a kid. "Take a picture and send it."

"I will, as soon as I get my lipstick on."

"Pink, I presume."

"What else?" She made a silly kissing sound. "I love you, Daddy. Have fun at the gallery opening tomorrow."

"I didn't say I was going."

"Well, you should. It's just your sort of thing."

He sidestepped her encouragement. "I love you, too, kissy Kaley. Be good."

"Okay. Talk to you later."

They said goodbye and as he ended the call, a big jolt of emptiness consumed his heart. But that didn't stop him from dialing Dana to decline her offer.

"Hello?" She answered in an eager tone. Hoping, perhaps, that it was him on the other end?

"Hi. It's Eric."

"Oh, I'm so glad you called, especially now. I've been trying on clothes for our date, just in case you say yes. I want to look amazing and blow you away."

Eric winced. She was too young and sweet for the likes of him. "I just talked to my daughter. She said that she was wearing a pink gown and a tiara to a Valentine-themed party. She's supposed to send me a picture."

"How fun. I'll bet she's going to have a great time. The gallery opening is Valentine art."

"I'm not going to go, Dana."

"Come on. Don't bail on me. Please. I really want to have a nice evening with you."

"I'm just not up for it."

A smile sounded in her voice. "How about if I send you a picture of what I'm going to wear?"

In spite of himself, he laughed. "I'd rather be surprised."

"Does that mean you're going to go?"

Did it? He glanced at the photos on the fireplace mantel, particularly the one from his wedding. Corrine had been an incredibly beautiful bride with her traditional white dress and misty veil. They'd gotten married at the beach. She'd always loved the sand and the surf. He did, too.

"You're confusing me," he said.

"Confusing you into having some fun?"

Just confusing him in general. "What gallery is it?"

"It's a new one near the beach."

He glanced at the portrait again. "Which beach?"

"Santa Monica."

Eric's stomach clenched. The same one where he'd said his vows. Was this a cosmic joke? "Dana—"

"Please." She persisted again. "Just give me a chance. One date. One kiss afterward."

A kiss? Now that was all he was going to be thinking about. He'd already been thinking about it at the diner, too. Could she tell? Did she know? Had he been that obvious? "You don't play fair."

"A little romance never hurt anyone."

Romance had hurt him plenty. In the picture, he was

standing barefoot on the shore in his tux, with his pant legs rolled up past his ankles, holding his new bride in his arms. He remembered scooping her up and making her squeal.

Dana said, "I really want to kiss you."

He wanted to kiss her, too. He wanted to put his mouth against hers and forget how lonely he was. "This is dangerous."

"It's a date, Eric."

"And a kiss," he reminded her.

"Just one at the door," she reminded him. She wasn't offering a night of unbridled passion.

Nor was he expecting anything like that. But maybe it was time for him to get back into the casual dating pool. Besides, Dana was about as sweet as they came. He couldn't ask for a nicer person to spend a few hours with. "Okay." He held his breath. One date. One good-night kiss. Plus Valentine art in Santa Monica. He prayed he could handle it. "I'll go out with you."

Her voice beamed. "You won't regret it. We're going to have a wonderful time. I'm so excited. Here, let me give you my address."

"I have to get a pen and paper." He went into the kitchen, away from the photo.

"Ready?"

"Sure. Go ahead." She rattled off her address and he wrote it down.

"It's the house in the back," she said. "You have to go through a side gate to get to it. But you'll see it when you get there."

"What time should I pick you up?"

"How about seven-thirty? The reception is from eight to ten."

"Okay." He was already nervous.

"My landlord will probably peer out her window to get a look at you."

"Is she a nosy old lady?"

"No." Dana laughed her lilting laugh. "She's young and beautiful, and I told her all about how yummy you are."

"Gee, thanks." More nerves. More of everything. "Nothing like putting a guy on the spot."

"You'll do fine. By the way, did you mention me to your daughter when you spoke to her earlier?"

"I told her that someone invited me to a gallery opening, but I didn't let on that it was a woman."

"Much less a twenty-six-year-old? Would you have told her about me if I was your age?"

"Probably not. I'm not comfortable talking about my personal life to my child, even if she sometimes pesters me about it."

"Pesters you how?"

"She wants me to start dating."

"What a bright kid. What's her name?"

"Kaley."

"Really? Did you know that Kaley means 'party animal' in the Urban Dictionary? Kaley is the name to have these days. It depicts the coolest girl ever."

"Then I guess we did her proud. Because she is the coolest girl ever."

"You're cool, too."

He shook his head. "Are you kidding? I feel like I'm in high school all over again."

"Because of me?"

"Yes. Because of you."

"So I make you feel young? That's good, isn't it?"

"I was a dork in high school."

She laughed. "Somehow I don't see you as ever being a dork."

"Believe me, I was."

"I'm surprised you can remember back that far."

He cracked a smile. "Smarty."

"I'll see you tomorrow."

"Yeah, you, too."

"I'm going to wow you with my outfit."

He would probably be predictable, in jeans and a sports coat. "Bye, Dana."

"Bye, handsome."

They hung up, and he marveled at how easily she flirted. He'd never met anyone like her.

He checked his emails on his phone to see if his cool kid had sent the picture. She had, and the image was funny and cute, with his daughter making a duck face. Her sparkly pink gown was atrocious. The tiara was tacky, too. But that was the point, he supposed.

He thought about Dana, wondering just how she planned to wow him. Tomorrow night was going to be a long wait.

Especially with that kiss looming in his mind.

Chapter Two

Eric drove to Dana's place and parked at the curb. She lived in a cozy, tree-lined neighborhood. The bungalow house in front boasted 1930s appeal with a sloping roof, a stucco exterior and a stone walkway. He assumed that was where her landlord lived. He didn't see anyone peering out from behind the lacy curtains, but that didn't mean he wasn't being watched.

He picked up her gift from the passenger's seat and got out of the car. He'd stopped by the florist and gotten Dana an orchid because of her obvious love of flowers. But suddenly he'd realized he'd made a mistake. Not necessarily for Dana, but for himself. Corrine's wedding bouquet had been made up of the same type of orchids.

How could he have overlooked that? Eric scowled. Maybe he hadn't. Maybe it was deliberate. As to why, he couldn't be sure. But it didn't sit well with him.

He headed for the side gate Dana had mentioned and opened the latch. Her yard was an explosion of greenery and festive blooms. Her tiny house sat amid the garden, which also contained a three-tiered fountain.

He knocked on her door. She answered and sent his libido into a tailspin.

She had the wow factor.

She'd donned a white dress with a bold red print. The slim-fitting garment hugged her in all the right places and was just low enough in front for him to see how bountiful her breasts were. Her shoes, a pair of flesh-colored heels, added about three inches to her height, elongating her already shapely legs. But what really enticed him was her hair. He'd never seen it loose, and tonight it tumbled around her shoulders in a mass of golden waves, making him itch to touch it.

Her makeup was stunning, as well, her eyes lined in a manner that reminded of him of an old-time movie star. Her lips were painted the same shade as the print on the dress, which he now realized were red dahlias. Instead of wearing a flower in her hair, she was wearing them on her dress.

"You look incredible," he said.

"Thank you." She spun around and showed him every curve. "I primped for hours."

"It paid off."

"Is that for me?" she asked.

The accidental orchid. "Yes." He handed it to her.

"Thank you. It's beautiful." She hugged it to her chest, much too close to her heart. "Come in, Eric."

As he entered her home, she put the potted plant on the windowsill, where a host of herbs created a fragrant mixture. Everything in her young vibrant world was tuned to the senses. A mosaic-topped café dining table was paired with mismatched chairs, and a mint-green loveseat that served as her sofa was bursting with tassel-trimmed pillows. A wooden coat rack held a collection of fringed shawls, and glass lamps were draped with feminine scarves.

"You have flair," he said. "This is like an antique gypsy cart." *Gypsy included,* he thought.

"Oh, thank you. I always thought it would be exciting to be an artist, but I don't have any talent in that regard. So I try to make up for it by keeping artistic things around me."

Did she keep artistic men around her, too? Was that part of her attraction to him? By most creative standards, Eric was on the conservative side. But he still fit the bill, he supposed, with his art-teacher vibe.

"You could be an interior designer," he told her.

"Really? Do you think so? That's something to consider. I'm torn about what to be when I grow up." She flashed her twentysomething smile. "If I ever do grow up."

"Being grown-up is overrated." Nonetheless, he was as grownup as it got. "Are you ready to head out?"

"Sure. Just let me get my wrap." She removed one of the shawls from the coat rack. They weren't just for show.

Before they exited her yard, she led him to the fountain. "Isn't he adorable? He's one of the reasons I want to see the Valentine art show. I love angels, and cherubs are my favorite."

He studied the statue in question. "People often mix cherubs up with putti. Unless you know the origins of the art, sometimes it can be difficult to tell."

She made a face. "I have no idea what you're talking about."

"Putti is plural for putto. They're childlike male figures, predominantly nude, and sometimes with wings."

"So what's the difference?"

"Cherubs appear in a religious context and are angels, whereas the genesis of putti is mythical or secular, like Cupid."

"So what is Tinkle?"

"Tinkle?"

She gestured to the fountain, and he smiled. She'd named the little guy after his antics. "I'd say he's a putto. They're prone to naughty deeds."

Dana laughed. "And here all this time I thought he was a misbehaving angel."

Eric laughed, too. "I'm sure we'll see plenty of cherubs at the gallery. And putti, too."

"It will be fun trying to tell the difference. We can make a guessing game out of it."

They walked to his car, and he opened the passenger side and watched her slide onto the seat. She was fluid and graceful, and he was still hoping that he could handle their date.

He got behind the wheel, and she gave him the address of the gallery. He typed it into the navigation system and drove into the night.

They barely spoke on the way. Mostly they listened to the female computer voice giving directions.

Finally Dana said, "I don't have one of those. I just take the chance of getting lost. Besides, sometimes you end up in interesting places when you go the wrong way."

"Do you have a bad sense of direction?"

"The worst." She grinned like an imp. "That part of my brain never developed, I guess. But we all have something not quite right about us."

His "not quite right" was his attraction to her. She didn't make sense in his organized world. She was too young, too free, too far from his norm.

They arrived at their destination, and he drove around to find a parking space.

"I love this area," Dana said.

Eric kept quiet. He used to love it, too. The ocean-front hotel that hosted his wedding was nearby.

He nabbed a parking spot, and they walked a block or so to the gallery.

They entered the reception area, where food and drink were being served. But they didn't make a bee-line for the buffet. To do so would have been tacky and insulting to the artist, or, in this case, the group of artists being showcased. Eric did opt for the bar, though. He needed a drink. Dana accepted a glass of wine, as well.

Together, they wandered around. The Valentine theme played out in different ways. Some pieces were warm and whimsical, others deep and epic. One spicy collection presented a sensual tone, whereas another was tragic.

The tragic art impacted Eric the most. Love found, love lost. He was morosely drawn to it.

Dana stood beside him as they gazed at a painting of a man reaching toward the sky, where a woman was fading away from him. The emotion it evoked hit him square in the gut.

"Have you ever been in love?" he asked her.

"No, but I hope to fall madly in love someday. It must be an incredible feeling."

"It is."

As he continued to study the piece, she studied him. He could feel her blue eyes burning into his soul.

"I'm sorry if this is difficult for you," she said softly.

He denied his pain. "I'm fine." He turned away from the painting. "Do you want to sample the buffet now?"

"Sure. That sounds good. But afterward, I'd like to go through the other parts of the exhibit again."

The other parts. The non-tragic works. "And play a cherub/putto guessing game?" They hadn't done that yet. There had been too much to look at, too much to take in, especially with Eric spending so much time on the sad images.

"Yes, I want to see the cherubs and putti again, but I want to take a closer look at the sexy artwork, too." She flashed her scarlet-lipstick smile. "I wasn't expecting to see that sort of thing included in the show."

Her mouth looked downright lush. To keep his brain from fogging, he tried to say something intelligent. "Sex is an important aspect of love."

"And sometimes sex is just sex. That's the only kind I've known. Not that I'm an authority on the subject or anything. I've only had a couple of boyfriends. Men I liked, but didn't love, obviously."

"I used to have uncommitted sex before I met Corrine. I barely remember those affairs now. But it was ages ago."

"Time slips by."

"Yes, it does."

He led Dana to the buffet, and they put appetizers on their plate. He tried not to watch her eat. But it was impossible not to be fascinated by her mouth. The kiss they'd promised to exchange was still imbedded in his mind.

She nibbled on an array of fruit. As his attraction to her heightened, he said, "You could be an artist's muse, looking the way you look tonight."

"Thank you. I think it's the nicest compliment a man has ever paid me."

"Young and nubile, as they used to say."

"You better stop talking like that or you're going to turn me into a seductress."

She was already a seductress, tempting him with her beauty and flair. He swigged his drink, doing his damnedest to cool off. They finished their food and wandered the gallery once more. He wasn't looking forward to seeing the sensual art again, not with the way she was affecting him.

The cherubs and putti were first, and he forced himself to play their game, comparing two illustrations that hung side by side. "So, which is which?"

"That's a cherub," she replied, about a heavenly-looking little guy. "And those are putti," she added, referring to the other drawing, where mischief ran amuck.

"How about that one?" He gestured to a painting that wasn't as easy to define.

She gazed at it for a while. "I don't have a clue."

"Truthfully, I don't, either. Sometimes it's tough to know what the artist is trying to convey."

They moved onto the sensual art, where lust reigned supreme.

Dana approached an alluring picture. "Look how beautiful it is."

Eric *was* looking. He wished he wasn't, though. The image was a photograph of a bewitching redhead reclining on a satin-draped bed with her hair coiled around the pillow and shaped into a heart. A tall, leanly muscled man tossed red dahlias onto the bed, only he was in shadow, his presence adding an air of mystery.

"I think she's dreaming about him," Dana said. "And that he's not really there."

Eric could see why Dana was attracted to this piece, especially with the inclusion of the dahlias. It made him want to kiss her, here and now, but it was neither the time nor the place, not when they'd agreed on a good-night kiss at her door.

He said, "The flowers are the same as what's on your dress."

"I noticed that, too. I can imagine being her, lying in bed, thinking about my lover. If I had a lover," she amended.

To keep from envisioning her in the same pose as the model, he asked, "Why do you wear flowers in your hair at work?"

"They make me feel happy, bright and pretty. I always wear them at my right ear because I read somewhere that it means a woman is available. Once I switch to my left ear, it will mean I'm taken."

"Remember the rose you gave me on the day I told you that I was a widower?"

She nodded.

"I took it to Corrine's grave. I try to bring her flowers when I can. It's weird, though, because I've probably given her more flowers in death than I gave her in life."

"I've never been to a funeral or a cemetery or anything like that. No one close to me has ever died."

He'd seen more than his share of death. "You're lucky."

"I'm lucky to be on this date, too. And I love that you brought me an orchid."

"I probably shouldn't be telling you this, but I think it's only fair to say it. Corrine's bridal bouquet had orchids in it. But I'm not sure if I chose it for that reason or it was subconscious."

"You said yesterday on the phone that I was confusing you. I guess that holds true for tonight, too."

"So it seems."

She smiled her usual smile. "I still love that you gave me the orchid."

"You don't care that I'm confused?"

"I just want you to be enjoying yourself."

Strangely enough, he was. "When we leave here, do you want to go for a walk on the pier?" Confusion aside, he wasn't ready for the evening to end.

Dana breathed in the sea air. Although a few of the restaurants remained open, most of the shops were closed. The connecting amusement park was shut down for the night, too, keeping winter hours.

"Did you know that this pier opened in 1909?" Eric asked.

"I knew it had been here awhile, but I didn't know the exact era. How different it must have been back then."

"I've seen old pictures of it with the men wearing suits and the women in long dresses. People used to fish here, too. Of course, they still do."

She nodded. She'd noticed people fishing on previous visits.

He said, "On a clear day, you can see Catalina Island. I used to spend a lot of time here as a kid." His hair blew across his forehead. "I even got married near here. The ceremony was on the beach."

"That sounds beautiful." She watched the nighttime waves crash onto the shore, the wind whipping across the water. She didn't mind that he talked about his wife. She was actually touched by how easily he confided in her about Corrine. "How old were you?"

"Twenty. We got married while we were in college."

She tried to picture him at that age and decided that he probably looked pretty much the same. Some people didn't change dramatically. Dana's mother had, but Mom had lived a tough life.

He said, "After we graduated, we pursued similar career paths. Me as a teacher and her as a youth counselor."

"You had a lot in common."

"Right from the start."

The breeze blew a little harder, fluttering the fringe on her shawl.

"Are you cold?" he asked.

"I think the air feels good." Being in his presence made her warm. She was wildly attracted to him: his tall, dark appearance, his cautious mannerisms. She especially liked the way he looked at her when he wasn't aware that she was stealing glances at him. She could only imagine how he used to look at his wife. She'd never known anyone who'd seemed to be that much in love. Eric was so deep and intense, so different from Dana. She'd seen how strongly the tragic artwork at the gallery had affected him. It was odd, too, how this date was playing out, with them ending up at the same beach as where he'd gotten married.

"Are you hungry for dessert?" he asked, his voice

cutting into her thoughts. "Or do you want a cup of coffee or a soda or anything?"

"I wouldn't mind having a milkshake. Chocolate always does the trick for me."

"I think the soda fountain place is getting ready to close. But I'll hurry and nab you one."

He left her standing at the rail with her shawl billowing and her mind on his wedding. She was also thinking about her own life and the part of her future that mattered most to her family.

When he returned with her milkshake, she thanked him, took a sip and said, "I want to get married and have kids someday. I promised my mom that I would never repeat our family history."

"What history?"

"Of unwed mothers. My mom was a single mother and so was her mother. It's not a very romantic legacy. Women raising children by themselves."

He frowned. "Why weren't the dads involved?"

"I was the product of a one-night stand so I have no idea who my father is. That was the only time Mom had ever done anything like that, and she's ashamed of her behavior, even until this day." Dana drank more of her milkshake, taking comfort in the chocolate. "She loves me and she's been a good parent, but there was still shame attached to my birth."

"I'm sorry."

"My grandmother's story is worse. She slept with a married man and that's how she got pregnant with my mom. She had a reputation for being a loose woman in her day, but it wasn't true. He'd seduced her into believing that he would leave his wife for her, and she paid the ultimate price when he spurned her afterward and refused to claim the baby. So you can see why they're pinning their hopes on me to have children the legitimate way. Mom calls their experiences sins of the past."

"I don't think there's anything sinful about having babies."

"Me, neither. But I still don't want to be an unwed mother. It would crush my family. Actually, it would probably crush me, too. I felt tainted as a kid, and I'd never want my child to feel that way."

"I'm sorry," he said again. He reached out as if he meant to stroke her cheek, but he lowered his hand before contact was made. After a moment of silence, he added, "My daughter's birth parents weren't married. They were only sixteen when she was born."

Confused, Dana blinked. "Her birth parents?"

"We adopted Kaley."

She couldn't hide her surprise. "All this time I thought she was yours."

"She is mine."

Dana apologized for the gaffe. "I didn't mean it that way. It just wasn't what I expected to hear."

"That's okay. There's no way you could have known," he quietly explained. "Corrine was adopted, so when we discovered that she couldn't conceive, we turned to adoption, too. Only Corrine wanted an open adoption for our baby because hers had been closed and she always felt a sense of loss not knowing who her birth parents were."

"So Kaley's adoption was open?"

"No. It didn't work out that way. But Corrine encouraged Kaley to search for her birth parents if she ever felt the need. And recently, she did. Kaley found her birth mother, and soon after that, she met her birth father."

"Wow." Intrigued, Dana tilted her head. "How did that go?"

"Remarkably well. For everyone. Not only did they embrace Kaley and welcome her into their lives, they got back together. They're getting married this summer. Kaley is going to be the maid of honor and I was asked to be the best man."

"That's a beautiful story." Homey, romantic. "Things don't usually happen that way." Or she assumed they didn't. All she knew was her own fatherless family. "I used to wonder about my dad when I was kid. Sometimes I still do. But I could never search for him. The only thing my mom knew about him was his first name. John. Can you imagine me trying to hunt him down?"

"That would be next to impossible, unless your mom was able to remember anything else about him that might lead you in his direction."

"She doesn't like to talk about him, and there's no point in putting her through that or making her relive what she considers her shame. Of course I compensated by becoming a bohemian." She flapped her fringe and made him smile. She shared her milkshake with him, too.

He drank from the straw and handed it back to her. "Where did you grow up?"

"You're going to laugh when I tell you."

"Why would I laugh?"

"Freedom, Ohio."

As predicted, he laughed. "You're from a town called Freedom?"

"Yep. The girl who's determined to be free. Actually, there are lots of Freedoms scattered throughout the States, but mine just happens to be in Ohio."

"When did you move to California?"

"After I graduated from high school." She glanced at the ocean again. The waves were getting bigger. "When I was about twelve, we came to Southern California for a vacation. I made up my mind then that I was going to live here someday."

"Is your mom still in Ohio?"

She nodded. "My grandmother, too. Neither of them ever got married. They'll probably go nuts when I get engaged."

He smiled. "The bohemian bride."

"Marriage is going to be the only traditional thing I'll probably ever do." They shared the last of her shake, and she got tingly putting her mouth where his had been.

"I'm glad I went on this date," he said.

The tingly feeling went off the charts. "It's not over yet. You still have to kiss me at my front door."

"That's pretty much all I've been thinking about."

Her, too. "The buildup is exciting."

"I hope I don't let you down."

"You won't." She was certain of it.

And she was right. Later, he took her home, and they stood on her stoop, with a fairy-tale moon in the sky. Eric moved closer, and her heart pounded up a magical storm. As he took her into his arms, she went downright goose-bumpy.

She was going to be kissed the way she longed to be kissed: tenderly, deeply, thoroughly. They'd been waiting all evening to make this happen.

It started off slowly, a flutter of sweet warmth. She wrapped her arms around him, basking in the strength of his body. She parted her lips, and their tongues met and mated.

Then things got hotter.

Dana moaned and pressed tighter against him. He slid his hands down her spine, resting on the curve of her rear. Her moan turned to a mewling, as they continued to kiss like hedonic fiends.

She rubbed against his fly. He swore beneath his breath, but that only made it better. He backed her roughly against the door.

A gust of wind rustled through the yard. She could hear it stirring the plants and flowers. Dana had the wicked urge to remove her dress.

"Stay with me," she heard herself say.

"I can't," she heard him reply.

"Yes, you can," she countered. They were whispering in between lusty sips of each other.

He groaned and ended the kiss, but his pelvis was still fused to hers. "Do you know what you're asking me to do?"

"Yes." She knew exactly what she was suggesting.

"I couldn't promise more than one night, Dana."

"It's okay, as long as I get to be with you." For now, all she wanted was him warm and naked in her bed.

"It would be too much like what happened with your mom."

"It's nothing like that. You're not a stranger. I know more about you than your first name. And we're going to be responsible. I have a whole box of condoms in my nightstand drawer."

"We still shouldn't."

"Why? Because of our age difference? We're both consenting adults, and I've been fantasizing about you since I met you." Fantasies she wanted to make come true.

She turned and unlocked the door. Determined to

have him, she reached for his hand, beckoning him to be wild and free with her.

And have the night of their lives.

Chapter Three

Eric went inside with Dana, but he didn't jump into the sweet flame of desire. He needed to slow down, to take a deep breath, to be absolutely positive that she understood his uncommitted position. He rarely acted on impulse and this wasn't the time to start. Nor could he bear to take advantage of her.

"Are you sure you want to do this?" he asked, as they stood in her living room.

"I'm certain. If I wasn't, I wouldn't have invited you to stay with me."

"What if we don't go on another date again?"

"You already said that you couldn't promise anything other than one night."

"How would you feel afterward if I stopped coming to the diner?"

She flinched a little. "Why would you do that?"

"Because it might interfere with our lives. And if it does, then I might not come back." He was giving himself an out, but he knew that he needed one. "If I keep coming to the diner, we might be tempted to do this again. And I don't think that would be a good idea."

"Stop worrying, Eric. I can handle this, however it turns out. I get that you don't want to enter into a relationship. But honestly, you can still eat at the diner." She sent him a teasing smile. "I won't serve you a side of sex with your meat loaf."

He couldn't help but laugh. She was a silly delight. "Can you imagine if that was on the menu?"

"It's on the menu tonight." Like the seductress she was, she dropped her shawl and removed her dress, giving him a sample of what he'd just ordered.

Heat. Hunger. A sensual agreement. She'd just assured him that she could handle a one-night affair, and he could no longer resist her charms, making him crazy hot.

She was crazy beautiful. He couldn't wait to touch her. She tossed the dress on the sofa and it landed in a pool of fabric dahlias.

She stood before him in her panties and bra and high heels. The longing to caress her, to feel the silk and softness of a woman engulfed him even more. He could barely breathe. She looked as if she were holding her breath, too.

"Are you ready?" she asked.

He nodded. He was more than ready. He wanted to drag her into his arms and sweep her into bed. Only it was her bedroom. Her house. Her rules.

She came forward and kissed him, much too softly.

It was all he could do to stop from going caveman. The years he'd been celibate felt like a lifetime.

"Let's go," she whispered, and took him to her room.

It was a girlish mess, with clothes all over the floor. Her sheets were rumpled, too. He'd never seen such pretty chaos. Amid the clutter was more of her gypsy styling, with embroidered pillows and lacy doodads.

She shrugged, smiled. "I wasn't expecting company in here. But I hardly ever make my bed, anyway." She gestured to the clothes on the floor. "Those are from last night, when I was figuring out what to wear for our date."

"And now here we are." Only minutes from being naked together. He took off his jacket and draped it over a chair.

"I'll get the protection so it's handy when we need it." She kicked off her shoes, crawled onto the bed and dug around in her nightstand drawer, leaning over with her rump in the air.

He doubted that her provocative pose was deliberate. She just seemed focused on her task. And damned cute while doing it.

"Shoot," she said. "I can't find them."

Just as Eric was thinking that he'd better dash out to buy some, she turned around. "Maybe they're in the bathroom. Give me a sec."

Off she went to continue the search. He was still preparing to go to the store, if need be. She was cute, but she wasn't very organized.

She reappeared with a grin. She'd found them. In fact, she held them up like a trophy. He'd never been so glad to see a box of rubbers.

He got rid of his shoes and joined her in bed, anxious to get his hands on her. She was anxious, too. She started undressing him, tugging at his clothes with feminine fury.

Once they were both bare and pressed together, he buried his face against her neck and breathed her in. Sweet heaven. Was it his imagination or did she smell like his favorite dessert?

"Am I crazy?" he asked.

"What?"

"I could swear you smell like cherry pie."

She smiled, her lipstick lustfully smeared. "It's cherry blossom perfume. I wore it just for you."

"I didn't notice it until now." But damn, he was glad that she'd sprayed it on her skin. "If I had some ice cream, I'd gobble you up a la mode."

She put her hand between his thighs. "If you had some ice cream, I'd let you."

He felt as if he was going to explode. Had he ever been this aroused? They rolled over the bed, tangling the bedding more than it already was. They did thrilling things to each other, too.

Hot, wild foreplay.

He grabbed for the condoms, tore into one and put it on. Dana arched beneath him, eager and willing. He saw the fire in her eyes, so blue, so blazing, so enticing.

Fast and furious, they made hammering love. He couldn't slow down if he tried. But she obviously didn't want him to. She matched him, stroke for heart-thundering stroke.

They reached the peak together, or that was how it seemed. He couldn't be sure. He was too blinded by his own hunger to gauge her orgasm.

By the time it was completely over and they separated, they were beaded with sweat and staring up at the ceiling, their fingertips still touching.

"Wow," she said.

"Double wow." He turned to look at her. "That was fun."

"Just as it was supposed to be." She planted a soft little kiss on his shoulder.

Now that it had ended, her affection made him uncomfortable. But most women got cozy afterward, he supposed, so why would she be the exception? He told himself that it didn't mean anything.

Eric got up and used her bathroom to dispose of the protection. He returned to Dana, and her tousled blond hair made him smile. He'd run his hands through it during their foreplay. He'd messed it up but good.

"Will you stay the night?" she asked.

"Sure. Why not?" He got back into bed with her. His discomfort had lessened. Besides, she deserved to be cuddled. To leave her alone now would have been disrespectful.

She said, "I can't wait to tell Candy how amazing my date with you was."

"Candy?"

"My landlord."

"You're not going to tell her you slept with me, are you?"

"Of course I am. That's a major part of how amazing it was."

"Why are girls allowed to kiss and tell and boys aren't?"

"Boys tell plenty."

"I never have."

"You're one of the good ones."

He didn't consider himself good or bad. He simply was what he was. "I'm just private about things like that."

"Candy is different from most girls. She hardly says anything about herself. She's divorced and is having a tough time with it. But she hasn't told me any of the details."

"It takes time to get over someone." He frowned. "I've heard that divorce can be as traumatic as what I went through. They say it's like death, only without the body."

"I've never thought of it like that before. But I never had cause to think about it before now. Candy is the only divorced friend I have." She nuzzled closer. "And you're the only widowed person I know. I'm so sorry you lost the woman you loved."

"I appreciate that you're able to discuss it with me without acting strange. I learned early on to keep most of it to myself. But with you, it's been easy."

"Maybe it's because I'm so easy." She nudged her nakedness against his and laughed at her own bawdy joke.

Such joy. Such innocence. He envied her that. "Someday some young guy is going to fall desperately in love with you."

She made a dreamy sound. "I hope so."

"It'll happen. Mark my words."

"Marking them now." She grabbed a pen off the nightstand and wrote L-O-V-E on her stomach.

He poked a finger into her navel. "That looks like a really bad tattoo."

"That's what we should do if we ever see each other again. We should get tattoos. A hunky guy like you should have something tribal and a bohemian girl like me should have something…" She seemed to be at a loss when it came to knowing what she should have.

He went ahead and made a few suggestions. "How about something flowery? Like cherry blossoms? Or something magical? Like a unicorn or a winged tigress?"

"Those are great ideas. I think I like the tigress the best." She purred playfully at him.

"That's sweet. But tigers don't purr. They chuff, like this." He made a breathy snort, mimicking the big cats.

"Oh, that's sexy. Maybe you should get the tiger tattoo."

"I think we should get some sleep." He adjusted his arm, giving her room to nestle in the crook of it.

She accepted his invitation and closed her eyes, and he watched her until she dozed off. He couldn't help it. He simply liked looking at her.

Dana expected Eric to awaken first, but she beat him to it. She discovered him, rough and rugged, and conked out beside her. His straight dark hair was spiked against the pillow and his jaw bore a bit of whisker stubble.

She scrounged around for a robe and found one in the midst of the clothing pile on the floor. It was her favorite robe, a silky number with a Hawaiian print.

After wrapping herself in it, she headed for the bathroom to wash what was left of last night's makeup off her face. She also brushed her teeth and put her hair in a twisty bun.

Then she went back into her room, sat on the edge of the bed and watched Eric come awake. He squinted at her, and she smiled.

"Morning," she said.

After a long stretch, he replied, "I've never been much of a morning person." There was a surly expression on his face.

"I'm an everything person," she told him, without losing her smile. "I like all times of the day."

He sat up a little straighter. "I need to go home."

"Not before breakfast." She didn't want him to leave just yet. She wanted to improve his mood. "Stay and eat with me. I'm a great cook."

"Really? You are?"

"Yes, sir. I'll whip up a batch of blueberry waffles. How does that sound?"

"Heavenly."

Perfect, she thought, commending herself. His mood was improving already. "How about eggs and bacon, too?"

"Even more heavenly. I'm a sucker for home cooking."

"In that case, I'll throw in some hash browns." The more food the better, especially if it was going to make him smile.

He did smile, and it warmed her all the way to her toes. He was still gloriously naked and gorgeous as ever.

He ran a hand through his hair. "Do you think I could use your shower? I'm never fully awake until I shower."

"Absolutely. Wash away."

"Any chance you have an extra toothbrush handy?"

"Are you kidding? I have a drawer full of toothbrushes in the bathroom. I have a ton of extra toiletries, too. There's a dollar store down the street and I go a little nuts when I shop there."

Another smile from the naked man. "Will you make coffee with breakfast?"

"Of course. That's a given." She watched him walk to the bathroom. All male. All healthy-guy muscle.

Dana went into the kitchen to whip up the meal. By the time Eric emerged, breakfast was ready. He'd obviously taken an invigorating shower. He looked refreshed. He was dressed, too, shoes and all.

She handed him a cup of coffee, and he inhaled the roasted aroma before he took a sip.

"This is better than the diner's coffee," he said.

"It's the same brand."

"It is? It takes richer."

"Maybe because it's more enjoyable to be drinking it at my house." She grinned. "Morning-after coffee."

"Maybe that's it. You look cute, by the way."

"Thanks." She was still in her robe. There didn't seem to be a reason to get dressed. She was comfy as she was.

They sat down at her table, and he thanked her for fixing the food. He ate with gusto. She smiled, glad that he'd agreed to have breakfast with her.

"Do you have any plans for the day?" she asked.

He shook his head.

"Me, neither. It's my day off." She waited for him to suggest that they spend the afternoon together, but he didn't say anything. Then again, she didn't really expect him to. Doing what came natural, she made the effort instead. "We ought to get those tattoos today, right after we finish eating."

"I'm not getting inked. But you go ahead."

"Not unless you come with me."

"I'm going home after breakfast, Dana."

"Come on, let's be spontaneous together. You can even help design my tattoo for me."

He shook his head. "I've been spontaneous enough for one day."

"This is day two."

"And I'm going home."

"Then what are you going to do?" She thought about what he'd said last night about not continuing to see each other. "Disappear and never be heard from again?"

"It's better that way, Dana."

"I think you'll change your mind." She batted her lashes. "You'll be back at the diner." She opened her robe and flashed him. "And you'll be back in my bed again, too."

He laughed. "You're something else."

It was wonderful to hear him laugh. "Yes, I am."

After breakfast, he kissed her goodbye. It was a warm, sexy, dreamy kiss, and Dana was certain he wouldn't be able to stay away. In her mind, they were meant to be lovers, for however long it lasted.

After he was gone, she sat outside by the fountain, excited about when she would see him again.

The days that passed turned into weeks, but there was no sign of Eric. Dana had been wrong. She hadn't charmed him into coming back to the diner, let alone sleeping with her again.

But that was the least of her worries. Or maybe it was the worst of them. Today she was a nervous wreck. Today she was confiding in Candy about her missed period.

Yes, Dana was late, and she'd never been late before. She could set a computer clock by her cycles.

"You better take a test," Candy said, as they sat in Dana's tiny living room, gazing at each other.

Dana shook her head. There had to be another reason for her missed period. She couldn't be pregnant. She just couldn't be. Not her. Not the girl who was determined to have babies the good old-fashioned married way.

"But we used a condom," she reiterated for the umpteenth time.

"Sometimes they fail." Candy blew out a breath. "Believe me, I know."

For a moment, Dana just stared at her. "Believe you? *You know?* What does that mean? Have you been pregnant before?"

Candy nodded, her past finally coming to light. "I was pregnant when I got married. That's why my ex asked me to marry him, for the sake of the child. He was from a proper family, and he felt it was important to do the right thing."

"What happened?"

"We were using condoms that were expired and didn't realize it. The latex gets brittle when they're old or improperly stored and they can have holes or tears in them that you're not even aware of."

"I was talking about what happened with the baby."

The brunette glanced away. "I miscarried."

That was what Dana assumed. "I'm so sorry."

"I was happy about getting accidentally pregnant. But after I lost the baby, our marriage just didn't work."

Because her husband hadn't loved her the way she'd loved him? Because without the baby, there was nothing keeping them tied together? To Dana, that seemed the obvious conclusion.

Candy said, "Why are we talking about me, when we should be concentrating on you taking that test?"

Dana fidgeted in her seat. Before she committed to

going to the drug store, she got up to the check the expiration date on the condoms.

Sure enough, they were old. Really, really old. Her situation was beginning to mirror Candy's.

Chance? Coincidence? Twisted fate?

Her anxiety accelerated. "If I am pregnant, Eric will never marry me." He would probably offer child support or whatever, but he wouldn't walk her down the aisle. "Not that I should marry him, anyway. We hardly even know each other." She rocked forward. "But how can I raise a baby by myself after the way I was raised? After the promise I made to my family?"

Candy gently replied, "You can always terminate if that's a better option for you."

She touched her stomach and recalled that she'd written L-O-V-E across it on the night she and Eric had made love. "I don't think I could do that." But the reality of being a single parent was knocking her upside the head, too. She understood the hardships it entailed.

Candy went to the pharmacy with her, and they looked at every kit on the market, reading the backs of the boxes. Dana couldn't decide which one to choose, so she let Candy decide for her. At this point, she couldn't think straight.

After they returned, Dana opened the box and read the instructions. The test was a digital model and was described as ninety-nine percent accurate. Curious to know everything, she even read the clinical stuff and how pregnant women produced a hormone called hCG, which was what the test would be detecting in her urine if she was pregnant.

Leaving Candy on the couch, Dana went into the bathroom and examined the test stick. According to the pamphlet, the words *Pregnant* or *Not Pregnant* were supposed to appear in the optical reader that was encased in the stick.

Anxious, she took the test. Then she sat in the living room with Candy and waited for the results, which was supposed to take all of three minutes. Normally that would have seemed like nothing, the amount of time to listen to a song or cook a frozen pizza in the microwave. But in this case, three minutes felt like an eternity.

Finally, her time was up and she returned to the bathroom to check the display and saw "Pregnant" on the screen. Candy saw it, too. Dana wanted to sink to the floor and cry, but she forced herself to remain standing and keep her eyes dry. Still, she was trembling inside. How could she tell her mom and grandmother? How could she deal with any of this?

"Maybe it's a false positive," she said. "Surely that sort of thing happens." She could hope, right? "I should probably see a doctor before I contact Eric."

She called to make the appointment, but the soonest she could be seen was three days away.

The days dragged by, with Dana praying her period would start. She could barely concentrate at work. She even mixed up people's orders, bringing them the wrong food.

She wasn't faring any better at home. Mostly she just sat around, worrying and waiting, without the slightest sign of her period.

By now she doubted that the test had been a false positive, but she was still going to the doctor to be sure.

The day of her appointment, Candy drove her there, with Dana fidgeting in the passenger seat. She was glad her friend was with her. She didn't know if she could have done this alone.

They arrived at the office and went inside. Dana signed in and they sat down and paged through outdated magazines.

Eventually Dana's name was called and she saw the doctor. He ran a blood test, and within an hour she had the results.

Positive. She was pregnant. *Unmarried and with child.* The very thing she'd promised her family would never happen to her.

On the way home, Candy kept shooting Dana worried glances, as if she expected her to cry. It was all she could do to hold herself together.

But as soon as they walked in the door, she lost it and burst into tears. Candy reached for her and she put her head against the other woman's shoulder and bawled her eyes out.

Candy kept saying, "It will be okay," but Dana knew that was just something to say. How was it going to be okay? How was she going to survive this?

After her horrific crying jag, she dried her face and blew her nose. Somehow, someway, it *was* going to be okay. She would do whatever it took to get through it, even if she bordered on falling apart.

Struggling to stay strong, she mentally prepared herself to call Eric and arrange a meeting with him. Relaying her news over the phone didn't seem right. She needed to tell him face-to-face that he was going to be a father.

Chapter Four

Eric couldn't fathom why Dana had called and insisted that he come to her house to see her. She'd claimed it was extremely important. In fact, she sounded nervous, even a little frantic, not at all like the easy-breezy bohemian girl he knew her to be. Her tone of voice had worried him. But this whole thing worried him. He didn't want to see her again. No, that wasn't true. He'd been thinking a lot about her since their date, and he'd been tempted to go back to the diner. But how could he do that without wanting her again? And if they got together again, then a relationship might ensue that he wasn't ready for. So he'd stayed away purposely, retreating to his cautious shell.

But now here he was, after work, parking his car in front of her house and hoping this wasn't a ploy on her part. A ploy for what? To seduce him back into her bed? No, he doubted that was it. Dana wasn't the game-playing type. Something was wrong, something she obviously felt the need to share with him.

He took the side gate to her place and found her sitting outside at her patio table, waiting for him. She looked pale and anxious. *Fragile,* he thought, his breath jerking from his lungs. She reminded him of Corrine when she'd first discovered that she was ill. Was Dana ill? Was that why she'd called him?

He wanted to turn and run, but he moved forward.

"Hi," she said softly.

"Hi," he replied, and noticed that she had a pitcher of ice water and two glasses on the table. Obviously she wasn't inviting him inside. Whatever she was going to say would be spoken here.

He sat across from her, and she poured him a glass of water. She poured one for herself and sipped it. Eric didn't reach for his. He wasn't thirsty.

"Tell me what's going on, Dana."

"I..."

His fear and worry increased. "Tell me, please."

She scooted in her chair, as if she were buying more time. "Okay, here goes." A slight pause, then, "I'm pregnant, Eric."

A haze of white flashed before his eyes. Was she suggesting that the baby was his? *No. No way.* They'd used protection. They'd been careful. It just wasn't possible.

Was it?

God, he hoped not. He prayed that the baby belonged to someone else. But if it did, then why was Dana telling him about it and not the other man?

He grabbed his water and swigged, afraid of what she was going to say next.

"The condom we used was expired, so I think that's how it happened. It probably had a tear in it or something. I didn't even think to check the date until…" Her words drifted into the breeze.

Eric just sat there, his mind spinning. His heart was palpitating, too. "It was me? It's mine?"

"Yes, of course it was you. Who else would it be? I haven't been with anyone since we were together. Or before that night, either." Her voice hitched. "I'm five weeks along."

He drained his glass. Their date had been five weeks ago. "And you're going to keep it?"

"Yes," she said again. "I haven't told my mother and grandma. I just haven't been able to bring myself to do that yet."

He nodded numbly. He didn't know what to do or say. He was forty-two years old and was having a baby with a girl nearly half his age. He didn't want to tell anyone, either.

Finally he managed, "I'll give you child support after it's born. I'll pay the deductible on your health insurance, too." Then he stopped to consider the type of job she had. "Do you even have insurance?"

"No, but I'm going to apply for state aide and see if I fall within the guidelines."

That sounded iffy to him. What if she didn't qualify? Or only qualified for partial coverage? "I'd rather that you had insurance. Just choose a provider and get some online quotes. Then I'll pay for the policy." He would have to dip into the last of his savings to cover it, but at least he still had a little money put away. "I want to be sure that you get consistent care."

"Thank you. I figured you'd offer to help however you could. You're a responsible man."

"Apparently not responsible enough. I feel terrible about being the one who did this to you."

"We really screwed up, didn't we? Especially me. Inviting you into my bed and providing an old condom."

"It's not your fault any more than it's mine. But I can't offer to marry you, Dana. I wish I could create the perfect scenario for you, but how can two people who barely know each other enter into a union like that? We'd be setting ourselves up for a really difficult situation."

"I know. I thought about that, too. How we hardly know each other. I didn't expect you to propose to me. Marriage isn't the answer."

He looked into the vastness of her eyes. Today they were a panicked shade of blue. He could see how scared she was of going it alone. "You vowed that you would never be a single mother."

"It's strange, isn't it? How life throws challenges at you? How a person's worst fears can come true."

It didn't seem fair, her being put in that position. He wanted to make it better for her, but short of marriage, which they'd just agreed wasn't the answer, he was at a loss to help her. "I'm so sorry, Dana."

"I'll be okay. I'll do whatever I can to make the best of it. I just need to focus on being a mom."

Eric had no idea how he was going to focus on being a brand-new dad, especially at this stage of his life. "I'm going to have to figure out a way to tell Kaley, just as you'll have to tell your family."

"I'm going to wait a while. I need time to build up to it."

"Have you told anyone else?"

"Candy knows. She was with me when I took the home pregnancy test. She went to the doctor with me, too."

Was that going to be his responsibility later? He hoped not. He'd seen far too many doctors and labs and hospitals during Corrine's treatment. He knew this wasn't the same thing, but he still didn't think he could deal with it. "I'm glad Candy went with you."

She clutched her stomach. "Do you think I'll make a good mom?"

"Of course you will." He was glad that she didn't say anything about him being a good dad. He wasn't making an emotional commitment to the baby, not like he'd done with Kaley. He feared that he didn't have it in him to be that kind of father again. Kaley was his heart. This baby was a mistake.

A poor little mistake.

"Candy wants me to keep living here. I want to stay, too. It will be cramped once the baby comes, but it's a nice safe place. I can make my bedroom into a nursery and sleep in the living room."

He knew that he should offer to create a nursery at his house, too, so the baby could spend weekends with him, but he couldn't see himself taking care of an infant again.

He couldn't see any of this. Although he wanted to do right by Dana, he felt like a zombie, going through the motions.

She said, "I'm going to keep working, of course. I'm going to stay in school, too, but I'm going to take on-line classes instead so I won't have to get a babysitter while I'm at school. I've been thinking about what you said about me being an interior designer. I might look into that."

"I meant what I said. You'd be good at it. It would be a nice career for you."

"I think so, too. And I can always waitress in between."

Eric thought about his coworkers and wondered what they would think of the situation he'd gotten himself into. He definitely wasn't the type of guy they would expect to be in this sort of predicament.

He considered Dana and what she was facing. It was going to be far more traumatic for her. She was the one who had to carry the baby, to give birth, to be the primary caregiver.

"I'm not kidding myself," she said, as if she were thinking the same thing. "It's not going to be easy trying to pull this off. But I figure it happened for a reason. Everything does, don't you think?"

No, he didn't. Otherwise his wife would still be alive. "My daughter tends to think that way. Ever since she found her birth parents, she's been hung up on fate."

"Do you think she'll think our baby is fate?"

Their baby. It almost made them sound like a couple. But they weren't. He and Dana would be living separately with Dana raising a child they'd conceived on a first date. How could that be fate? "I have no idea how she's going to react." He only knew how uncomfortable he was going to be revealing what he'd done and who he'd done it with.

"When are you going to tell her?"

"I don't know. This weekend, maybe. She's supposed to be coming home to visit me. I was going to take her out to her favorite sushi bar."

"That's nice. Can I see a picture of her?"

"What? Why?"

"Because she's going to be the baby's big sister."

He couldn't argue with her reasoning. What she said was true. Dana and the tiny life in her womb were connected to his daughter. One night of passion and he and Dana had created a child. It boggled his brain. When he was young and eager to start a family, he would have been thrilled to have made a baby so quickly and easily, but he was older and of a different mindset now. None of it made sense, not for him or for Dana.

He opened a file on his smartphone and showed her an image of Kaley.

"She's beautiful. She looks as if she could be your biological child."

"She's part Native on her birth father's side. That was instrumental in the adoption."

"I wonder what this baby is going to look like."

"Maybe it will favor you." He watched her hair blow across her cheek, thinking how pretty she was. "Or maybe it will favor both of us."

Dana smiled a little. "They're going to do an ultrasound at six weeks and give me a copy of the picture afterward."

"Are ultrasounds routine this early on?"

"They are with my doctor. He likes to do one at the beginning, then another one later when the baby is more developed."

At this stage, Eric imagined that the fetus was going to look like a peapod or some other odd shaped little thing. "Is Candy going to the ultrasound appointment with you?"

Dana nodded. "Candy was pregnant when she was

married, but she lost the baby. She told me on the day we discovered that I was pregnant."

"I'm sorry for her loss." Candy seemed like a good friend to Dana.

"I'll introduce you to her one of these times."

"I'm just glad she's there for you."

"Me, too. It helps me not to feel so alone."

Struggling to give her comfort, he reached across the table for her hand. She curled her fingers into his, but the contact wasn't as encompassing as it should have been. He wasn't any good at this.

"Are you sure you're going to be all right?" he asked.

"I'm certainly going to try."

He didn't know what he was going to do, other than combat the expectant-father panic. "I'm really sorry, Dana."

"You don't have to keep apologizing."

"I feel like I made a mess of things."

"That's just because you're nervous. So am I. We just need more time to let it sink in."

"Then if there's nothing else left to discuss right now, I should head home." He needed to sit quietly and breathe. His heart was punching the crap out of his chest.

"Okay." Her hand drifted from his. "I'll be in touch."

"Let me know about the insurance quotes."

"I will."

She walked him to the gate in the corner of the yard. They didn't hug goodbye. They didn't do anything but stand there, awkward as you please. He'd obviously failed to comfort her, the gentleness he'd offered much too fleeting. He definitely needed to go home, but he lingered a moment longer.

Finally he opened the gate and passed through it, glancing back one last time—at the beautiful young woman carrying his child.

Kaley arrived on Saturday. They went out for sushi and Eric worried the entire time, trying to figure out how to tell her his news when they returned to the house. On the drive back, he stared out the windshield.

His emotions were a freaking mess. Maybe he shouldn't tell Kaley this soon. Maybe he should wait until closer to the baby's birth.

No, that wasn't a good idea. It wouldn't be right to keep it a secret from his daughter. But damn, he wished that he'd never gotten himself into this situation.

And Dana. Sweet Dana. How difficult this must be on her. He remembered her saying that her being a single parent would crush her family and that she would be crushed by it herself, too.

So what did that make Eric? The man who'd crushed her?

He parked in the driveway, and he and Kaley went inside. He looked at her, thinking how lovely and grownup she was. Grownup enough to accept his news? God, he hoped so.

He took another look at her and realized that she had a similar style to Dana's. She favored gypsy-type clothes, too. Not as wild as Dana's, but similar nonetheless. Of course she and Dana were only eight years apart. They were practically the same generation.

"Kaley," he said.

"Uh-huh?" She removed her sequined flats and left them by the front door. Her sweater had a row of sequins on it, too.

He said, "I need to tell you something."

She tucked her hair behind her ear. Her long dark hair was sleek and straight with a hint of red that shone in the sun, courtesy of her birth mother.

She furrowed her brow. "Is something wrong? You've been kind of spacey all day."

Yes, something was very wrong. "Sit down, okay?"

"Now you're scaring me."

"It isn't scary." Not the kind of scary he knew she was thinking, like when Corrine had gotten sick.

She plopped onto the sofa, and he took the chair opposite her. "Okay, Dad, shoot."

He started off easy. "I went out on a date with someone."

"Really? Oh, that's great."

No, it wasn't. "I had relations with her, too."

"Relations? Seriously? That's so corny." She laughed. "So you slept with her? That's cool."

Again, it wasn't great or cool or any of that. "She's pregnant, Kaley. We messed up and she got pregnant."

His daughter's eyes went wide. She was stunned into silence.

He hastily added, "The protection was old and it failed."

More silence.

Eric felt as if he was heading to the gallows. Off with his head for being the man who'd crushed Dana and confused Kaley.

"You're having a baby?" she finally asked.

"Yes. She wants to keep it."

"Two old people having a kid. Who would have thought..."

Oh, cripes. Here came the rest of his admission. "She isn't old. She's only twenty-six."

Kaley's eyes went wide again. Super wide. "*Dad.* Oh, my God. *Dad.*"

"I know. It's crazy. She's a waitress at a diner where I used to eat, and she invited me on a date, and then I stayed the night with her. It was just that once. I knew she was too young for me. I knew better."

"When is the baby due?"

"I don't know."

"How can you not know?"

"She didn't tell me and I didn't ask. All I know is that she's around five weeks and they're going to do an ultrasound at six weeks."

"It's still really early."

"Our date was around Valentine's Day. It was the gallery opening I mentioned to you."

"Oh, yes. I remember that. So what's your baby mama's name?"

His baby mama? He didn't like that phrase. It was too carefree a depiction. "Dana."

"Is she nice? Will I like her?"

"Yes, I think you'll like her."

Eric could see her expression change as she mulled it over, an intrigued light glittering in her dark eyes.

"This is actually pretty exciting, Dad. I mean, first I meet my birth parents and now I'm going to have a little brother or sister. Are you and Dana going to start dating again?"

"No, Kaley, it isn't like that."

She gaped at him. "You're having a baby together, but you're not going to pursue a relationship?"

"I told you, she's too young for me."

"Come on, what's age? Only a number."

"I hate that saying."

"'Cause you're being a grump. At least try to rejoice in the baby you created."

"I don't know how to be a father again."

"Sure you do. Just do what you did with me."

"It isn't the same."

"How can you say that? You adopted me, a child who wasn't even your blood, and loved me and cared for me. How can you not love and care for the one your baby mama is going to have?"

"Quit calling her my baby mama."

"Fine. Dana, then. How does she feel about all of this?"

"Mostly she's just scared. She never wanted to be an unwed mother." As long as they were talking openly, he went ahead and relayed Dana's family history. He didn't see the point in keeping it a secret. "This is as bad for her as it is for me."

"As bad for her? It's worse. Way worse."

"You're right. It is." He'd already considered how traumatic it was for Dana. "But I can't make it better for her. I wish I could, but I can't."

"You could marry her, if she'll have you."

He couldn't believe what he was hearing. "Marriage isn't an option."

"Maybe you're supposed to think of it as an option. Maybe this baby is the Creator's way of filling that empty space in your heart. Mom is gone, Dad, and she's not coming back."

"I know she's gone." He knew that better than anyone. "I don't love Dana, and I'm not marrying a woman I don't love."

"They say that people can learn to love each other."

"I'm past the point of learning to love someone. I had the real deal."

"And you're going to wallow in it for the rest of your life? Mom wouldn't have liked that."

"Please don't talk to me about what your mom would have liked." He knew exactly what Corrine would be telling him to do. When she'd finally resigned herself to the fact that she was dying, she'd started in on him about moving on with his life after she was gone. So much so, they'd argued about it.

Kaley heaved a sigh. "I feel sorry for Dana. What if some guy did to me what you're doing to her? What if he was keeping himself detached from me and the baby I was going to have?"

That was something he prayed would never happen. "I'm going to help her pay for everything. I'm going to try to do what I can."

"That's not the same as being there for someone. I'll bet she would marry you if you asked her."

"I already told her that I couldn't, and she agreed that we shouldn't."

"I think she would reconsider."

"You don't even know her, Kaley."

"I know how girls feel. Need I remind you that I'm a girl? And if the worst thing in the world to me was being a single mom and the baby daddy offered to marry me, I'd do it."

Baby daddy. Baby mama. He'd told her to quit with that stuff. "Marriage isn't something someone should leap into."

"It's not fair that you get to control the situation."

"I'm not in control of anything." He was confused

and powerless, unsure of what the hell he was supposed to do. "You have no idea how this is affecting me."

"I think you're putting your needs before hers."

"You have no right to judge me."

"For being a jerk?"

"Okay, fine. I'm a jerk. I'm the worst expectant father who ever lived. But damn it, Kaley. Lay off me."

"I'm really starting to hate you right now."

"Yeah, well, go ahead." At the moment, he hated himself, too.

"Good. Fine. Hate it is." She stormed off to her room, slamming the door behind her.

Eric remained in his chair, lost in the mess he'd made of everyone's lives.

After an hour had passed, Eric knocked on Kaley's door.

She called out, "Come in," and he entered the room. It was the same room she'd had since she was a child, triggering memories of her when she was little, content in her kid-oriented world. The sugar-and-spice decor had changed since then, reflecting her age now, but he was remembering it as it had been.

She sat on her bed, with her knees drawn to her chest, her iPad beside her. She was always using an electronic device of some kind.

"I'm sorry," he said.

"I'm sorry, too." She gestured for him to come closer. "I don't hate you, Dad. I love you."

"I love you, too." He loved her with every ounce of who he was. "You're everything to me."

"The new baby should be everything, too."

"I just found out about it a few days ago. I need more time to accept what's happening."

"I know. It just bothers me that you seem so detached."

"I'll try to become more attached."

"I still think you should offer to marry Dana."

"Oh, Kaley." He sat down in her desk chair. "Life just isn't that simple."

"I think it can be, if you let it. Look at what happened with Victoria and Ryan."

Victoria and Ryan were her birth parents, and yes, they'd come a long way, but the circumstances were different. "It isn't the same."

"Ryan detached himself from me and Victoria when I was born."

"Because he was scared."

"You're scared, too."

"That doesn't mean I should marry Dana. And I already told you, she agreed that it wasn't the right thing for us to do."

"But it wasn't a legitimate offer. You didn't ask her to marry you. You didn't give her the opportunity to think about it."

"She probably already thought about it on her own."

"Only because she assumed it wasn't an option. At least if you ask, you'll have a chance to explore the subject. At least then you two can discuss it and see if it really could be a possibility."

He didn't reply. But he knew whatever he said wouldn't matter. Kaley was determined to sway him, and when she wanted something, she wasn't going to give up.

She said, "You're a traditional man, Dad. An honorable man. You shouldn't have a baby out of wedlock, and especially with a woman who vowed to never be a single mother."

"All right. So let's say for the sake of argument that I ask her and she agrees, and then we have a crappy marriage. How is that helping the baby?"

"At least the child will look back on his or her life and know that you tried to be a family."

"It's a nice notion, and your heart is in the right place, but I—"

"Please, just think about it. Even if Dana turns you down, at least you offered. At least she can tell her family that the man was willing to marry her."

"You're awfully committed to a woman you've never even met, Kaley."

"She's going to give birth to my brother or sister. I should be committed to making this easier for her."

"You and your women's causes."

"My minor is women's studies," she reminded him. "So what do you expect, for me to take the male perspective on this?"

"Even if the male perspective belongs to your father?"

"Especially if it belongs to my dad. I want to be proud of the way you're handling the situation."

As opposed to being ashamed of his detachment? Eric looked into her eyes. He wanted her to be proud of him. He wanted to be the man she believed him to be. He wanted to try to be that man for Dana and their baby, too, if that was possible.

He stood up, took a deep breath and told himself he could do this, no matter how scared he was. "I'll talk to Dana about it."

Kaley jumped off the bed and flung herself into his arms. "Thank you, Daddy."

He nuzzled her hair, thinking about the child in Dana's womb and how someday that little person was going to call him "Daddy," too.

"You won't regret it," she said.

He held his daughter a bit closer and hoped that she was right. Because if she wasn't, then Eric was about to embark on what could possibly be the biggest mistake of his life.

Chapter Five

Dana left the diner and walked out to the parking lot toward her car. She was exhausted—mentally, emotionally and physically. She wasn't having full-on morning sickness, but she'd had a few quick bursts of queasiness. A prelude, she supposed, of what was yet to come.

All she wanted at this point was to go home and sleep, and it was only 6 p.m. So far, being pregnant wasn't fun. Of course no one claimed that it would be. And being a single mom wasn't going to make it any easier. But what good would it do to keep reminding herself of that? It would only create more stress. And if she was stressed, then the baby would feel it, too.

Her sweet little illegitimate baby. A stigma Dana knew all too well. But who was she supposed to blame for history repeating itself? Herself? Eric? It wasn't his fault any more than it was hers. Still, raising this baby by herself wasn't an easy pill to swallow.

As she neared her car, she saw a tall, dark man standing beside it. Eric? Yes, Eric. She'd just been thinking about him and now there he was. His car was parked next to hers.

Nearly a week had passed since she'd told him about the baby, and he looked handsome as ever, with his chiseled features, casual clothes and masculine intensity. Dana was still attracted to him, but she wished that she wasn't. Having those types of feelings for him wasn't in her best interest.

Was he here to discuss the health insurance policy they'd talked about? She hadn't had time to get any estimates.

She hadn't had time to do anything, not even call her mom and grandmother. No, that wasn't true. She'd purposely avoided that. When it came to her family, Dana was burying her head in the sand.

"Hey," Eric said to her. "I was hoping we could talk."

"Here?"

"We can sit in my car." He lifted his hand and extended a tall paper cup with a straw sticking out of the lid. "I got you a milkshake. The best in the city, I think."

Was this her first pregnancy craving? Now she was hungry for exactly what he was offering: thick, creamy chocolate. "Better than the one we shared at the pier?"

"It's just as good. It's from an ice cream shop near where I live."

Dana snatched it up and took a long, satisfying slurp. He moved a little closer, and she frowned. She didn't want him crowding her.

He cleared his throat, then said, "I'm sorry that I didn't offer the security you and the baby deserve."

Confused, she sucked down a bit more of the drink. "You offered to pay child support. And cover medical expenses, too."

"That's not the kind of security I mean. I'm talking about emotional support. I talked to Kaley about you, and she opened my eyes to what I should have seen on my own. She thinks I should propose, and I agree with her that I should." His voice went soft. "I apologize for not having done it before now."

Oh, God. Dana's heart thumped. Dare she ask? Dare she make him say it? "Propose what?"

He made an old-fashioned gesture, bending slightly at the waist. "Marriage. Ask for your hand in matrimony." He righted his posture.

"Is that why you're here? To propose?"

"Yes, that's exactly why I'm here."

"I think I need to sit down." Suddenly she was feeling a tad dizzy.

Eric opened the passenger door to his car, and she slid onto the seat and told herself to breathe. He got behind the wheel. She rolled the milkshake cup across her forehead, grateful for its icy coolness.

"Are you okay?" he asked.

"I'm getting there." She lowered the cup. "Do you want to get married, Eric?"

"I want to do what's right, and you shouldn't have to be a single mom, not if I can do something about it." He paused as if he was collecting his thoughts. "I want to make it easier for you."

"You were reluctant to go on a date with me and now you're talking marriage. That's a huge step, Eric."

"Yes, it is, and I'm not going to lie and say that I'm not scared of being a husband and father again. But that doesn't mean that I won't do whatever I can to try to make it work with you and give our child two full-time parents."

Dana studied him: his candid expression, the anticipation in his dark brown eyes. He seemed sincere, but how could she be sure that he was emotionally equipped to back up his claim?

She thought about what he'd said about his daughter encouraging him to do this. "Why is Kaley so adamant about marriage? Does she think this is fate?"

"That's part of it. Also, I told her about your family history and she feels badly for you. Plus she's excited about having a brother or sister. She's already getting attached to the baby in her mind."

"Oh, that's nice." Dana cradled her stomach. "I'm attached, too. Afraid of what the future will entail, but attached."

"I was hoping that my proposal would help you feel less afraid. But you're still scared, just like I am."

Yes, she was. But regardless of either of their fears, she wanted to say yes, to jump at the chance to make their child legitimate, but she knew that she shouldn't leap headfirst into something an idealistic eighteen-year-old girl had cooked up. "I haven't told my family about the baby yet."

"Now you can tell them that the father proposed."

"They'll think I'm crazy if I decline your offer. Especially when they ask what you're like and I tell them that you're an attractive, hardworking, responsible man who already raised an adoptive child." They would think Eric was the catch of the century.

"You have to do what's right for you, not your family."

"I don't want to be a single parent, you know that. But I'm concerned about rushing into something that could cause both of us pain afterward." She met his gaze. "Marriage is difficult enough, let alone in a situation like ours."

"Kaley compared us to Ryan and Victoria. Her birth parents," he clarified. "It's not the same, but they still had major obstacles to overcome."

She remembered him telling her that Kaley's birth parents had reunited and were getting married this summer. She also recalled him saying how young they were when they conceived.

"When Victoria got pregnant, she and Ryan were in high school," he said, confirming what she already knew. "Their families convinced them that adoption was the only answer. But secretly Victoria wanted to keep the baby. She dreamed of marrying Ryan."

"Was she in love with him?"

"Yes. He loved her, too, but he didn't realize that he did, not until many years later. He was too mixed-up to sort out his feelings. But the one noble thing he did was promise to be there when the baby was born. Only he panicked when she went into labor and never showed up at the hospital. Victoria didn't forgive him, not until Kaley came back into their lives."

"Their background is nothing like ours. We aren't lovelorn teenagers. You were my customer at the diner and we had one sexy date."

"I know, but there was still a baby involved, and they didn't even get to keep theirs. At least we have the option of getting married and raising our child together."

Yes, they had that option. But Eric's daughter comparing them to Ryan and Victoria didn't help Dana feel better. Not when the other couple was in love, and she and Eric were nothing of the sort. That alone should be reason enough *not* to marry him. But the devastation of being a single parent was still weighing on her heart. "I'm grateful for your proposal. It's a very kind thing for you to do. But I need more time to think about it. I still have reservations about rushing into anything, for both our sakes."

"I understand. And I'll be here for you, either way. The best I can."

The best he could. That was all she could ask, wasn't it? For him to be a good father to their baby. And a good husband to her, too? She didn't know if that was possible.

She curiously asked, "What kind of wife do you think I'd make?"

"Let me see." He took a moment to respond. "I think you'd be sweet and funny. And busy. You'd always be jumping into some sort of scattered project. You'd be messy, too." He smiled. "You'd probably leave your clothes all over our bedroom."

She rolled her eyes. "You make me sound like a handful."

"Because you probably would be." He leaned over and bumped her shoulder. "Of course you do have that home-cooking thing going for you."

"A big point in my favor."

"A huge point."

At least there was something she did that he admired in a wife, although it did strike her as a bit chauvinist. "I should probably kick you to the curb right now."

"For appreciating your cooking? What's wrong with that?"

"Nothing. I'm just being sensitive, I guess. I didn't mean to overreact, and I'm glad you like my cooking."

Besides, she realized it was a stupid question anyway. He couldn't know what sort of wife she would make anymore than she could know what type of husband he would be.

There was a lot to consider, including his broken past. If Dana married him, would it be her job to try to fix him? Candy had already accused her of being drawn to troubled people.

"I think I should go home," she said, feeling overrun with the decision she had to make. "I'm tired from a long work day." She couldn't think about fixing the broken, not now, not while she was uncertain about her own future.

Before she reached for the door handle, he asked, "When is the ultrasound? You didn't have it already, did you?"

"No. It's tomorrow."

"Is Candy still going with you?"

"Yes. She'll be there."

"Will you let me know how it turns out?"

"I'll bring you the picture if you want to see it."

"When you first told me about the ultrasound, I thought about what the fetus was probably going to look like."

"What did you envision?"

"I figured it would look like a peapod or something."

"A peapod. Oh, that's cute. Maybe I'll start calling it Sweet Pea." She glanced down at her stomach. "What do you think, little one? Do you like Sweet Pea?"

He watched her with a kind of strange wonder, and she realized that this was as new to him as it was to her. He had a child, but he'd never been through a pregnancy.

He said, "Sweet Pea sounds like a girl. Do you think it's a girl?"

"I have no idea. But the Sweet Pea in *Popeye* was a boy."

"Ah, that's right. The cartoon baby. Maybe ours is a boy, too."

"We'll be able to find out later. Would you want to know ahead of time?"

"Would you?" He returned the question.

"If you do."

"We'll decide when the time comes."

"There are a lot of things to decide." First and foremost if she was going to accept his marriage proposal. "I better go now for sure. I really am tired."

She said goodbye and exited his car, taking what was left of her milkshake. When she got in her car and backed out of the parking space, Eric remained inside his vehicle, watching her as she drove away.

"Are you nervous?" Candy asked Dana, as they waited in her doctor's office.

"A little." But she knew that the ultrasound wasn't going to be painful. The only discomfort was her bladder. She'd been instructed to drink several glasses of water ahead of time because in first-trimester sonograms, a full bladder made the baby easier to see.

"Just don't think about Tinkle during the procedure," Candy said, teasing her.

They grinned foolishly at each other. Clearly, the

last thing she needed was to put the sound of the fountain in her head.

After the nurse called Dana's name and she was settled onto the examination table with her abdomen exposed, she glanced over at Candy. Her friend sat in a chair on the other side of the table.

The technician stood beside the computer, preparing to get underway. Soon Dana's stomach was covered in a cool gel, and while the technician slid the transducer back and forth, Dana watched the monitor.

Then there it was. Her baby.

She covered her mouth and stifled a laugh. It looked more like a kidney bean than a peapod. But she would be darned if she was going to start calling it Sweet Bean.

"Look at that," Candy said.

"I know. Sweet Pea is having its picture taken."

The technician smiled. She was young, probably about Dana's age.

"Do you have kids?" Dana asked her.

"Not yet."

"This is my first, and my friend Candy is going to be its godmother."

"I am?" Candy asked.

Dana turned away from the monitor to look at her. "Yes, you are. I couldn't be doing this without you." The drug store test, the doctor visits, the conversations they'd had. "You earned your godmother status."

"Then I'm honored to accept it. But don't downplay your strengths. You're doing just fine, mama, and you'll continue to do just fine. I'll bet Sweet Pea thinks so, too."

They both returned their attention to the screen and marveled at the baby.

When the ultrasound ended, Dana was given two black and white photos of her little angel. She and Candy chatted about the baby on the way home. They talked about Eric's proposal, too, even though they'd already discussed it at length earlier. Candy wasn't much help in that regard, other than telling Dana "to do whatever feels right."

After Candy left for work, Dana spent the remainder of the day milling around, then got a brainstorm. She drove to the pharmacy—the same one where she'd bought the pregnancy test—and purchased two pictures frames.

Once she was back home, she framed Sweet Pea's photos and placed one of them on her dresser. The other one was for Eric. She had no idea how he would feel about a receiving a framed image of a fetus, but she suspected that Kaley would appreciate it. She was grateful that his daughter was excited about the baby.

Dana still wasn't sure what to do about Eric's proposal.

She honestly didn't know what felt right. If she called her family for their advice, they would tell her to marry the father of her child. For them it would be a no-brainer.

Shouldn't it be a no-brainer for her, too? She'd promised her mom and grandma that she would never give birth to an illegitimate child. She'd made that same promise to herself.

So why was she dragging her feet? Was it because the proposal had been Kaley's initial idea and not Eric's? Or was it because there was no love involved?

Really, though, why should that matter? Dana wasn't expecting Eric to fall in love with her nor was she planning to fall in love with him. The idea was to give their baby a name and do the best they could to raise it together, for however long their union lasted.

So do it, she told herself. Go to his house, give him the picture and accept his proposal.

Having made her decision, she sat on the edge of the bed and laughed at the craziness of her situation. Go to his house? She didn't have his address. She didn't even know where Sweet Pea's daddy lived.

Dana glanced at the clock. It was after four. Was Eric home from work by now?

Instead of calling, she texted him: Can I stop by tonight to talk?

Soon her phone bleeped, signaling a reply: Yes. When?

You pick the time.

He came back with: 6 or so?

Ok. Need ur address.

The next reply took a little longer because he included directions, with a side note that said: So you and Sweet Pea don't get lost.

She answered with a smiley face. She was touched that he'd included the baby. She actually pressed the phone against her heart.

Refusing to make a fuss over her reaction, she lowered the phone. She had a right to be happy that Eric was starting to take an interest in their child. It made her feel better about bringing him the framed photo.

And it made her feel better about her decision to marry him, too. A bit more certain. A tad more convinced. A scooch more ready.

Lord, she was scared. But she wasn't going to back out. It would be far scarier to raise the baby by herself. Besides, now her family would be proud of her, the way Kaley would be proud of Eric. They would have everyone's blessing.

Dana reached for her phone again, only this time, to text Candy. The other woman wouldn't receive the message until after her classes ended, but Dana wanted to share her news just the same.

She wrote: Going to Eric's tonight. Going to accept. Think good thoughts for me. Will call Mom and Grandma tomorrow.

Around five o'clock, Dana got ready to go. Determined to look pretty for her acceptance speech, she blushed her cheeks, applied lipstick and fluffed her hair. Next she brightened up her outfit with a colorful scarf that she used for a belt, looping it through her jeans. Since it was a chilly day, she slipped on a pair of suede boots and an old fringed jacket she'd bought at a garage sale.

As she stood in front of the mirror, she thought about what Eric had called her on their date. *The bohemian bride.* Only when he'd said it, he'd been referring to her as someone else's future wife.

What kind of wedding would they have? How many guests would they invite? Would Mom and Grandma fly out to attend? Surely, they would find a way to afford the trip. Dana couldn't imagine them missing her nuptials.

Then, of course there was the matter of a dress. She would definitely shop for something vintage. Something wild and free. Something that reflected her style.

She was going to suggest that they get married sooner rather than later. She didn't want to have a swollen belly when she walked down the aisle. The bohemian bride didn't want to look like a pregnant bride, even if that was what she was.

At five-forty-five, she left for Eric's house. She hit a bit of traffic on the way, arriving late. But not too late, she surmised. He'd said six or so, and she was still within the "or so" range. Plus, she hadn't gotten lost. His directions were spot on.

His single-story dwelling was located in a properly maintained, typically suburban tract-housing neighborhood. The lack of individualism disappointed her, but she wasn't surprised by it. She'd pictured him in an area like this. What she hadn't pictured, up until this strangely reflective moment, was living here with him. But the white-and-gray house with its brick planter and neatly mowed lawn was going to be her home, too.

Dana rang the bell. She'd put Sweet Pea's photo in a previously used gift bag. She recycled ribbons and bows, too.

Eric answered the door, and her heart fluttered, like little feet bumping at her chest. Was that how it was going to feel when the baby was bigger and kicking against her belly?

"Come in," he said.

The house was painfully quiet. She would've preferred background noise, radio or a TV. But it was just the two of them, their voices echoing amid the silence.

Immediately, she glanced around, taking note of the polished oak furniture, surrounded by beige and blue accents. She suspected that a woman had originally decorated it, a woman who was neat and tidy and traditional.

"Is this the house you had with Corrine?"

"Yes. We bought it a few years after we were married."

"So this is where Kaley was raised?"

He nodded. "She still has a room here. There are four bedrooms altogether. One of them is my studio. I've always done a little freelance art on the side. Illustrations, logos, that sort of thing. We used to make Native American crafts and sell them at powwows, too."

"We?"

"Corrine, Kaley and me."

"Was Corrine Native, too?"

"No. She was Anglo, like you. Blonde, blue-eyed."

"Has that always been your type?"

He roamed his gaze over her, and she got tingly, her skin going warm, her attraction to him as strong as ever.

"I never really considered myself as having a type," he said. "But apparently I do."

Sexual tension. This was definitely an inopportune moment for it. Neither of them seemed to know what to say while it was happening.

When the eye contact got too uncomfortable, too quietly awkward, Dana glanced around again.

Amid the strained silence, she noticed that the fireplace mantel held a grouping of framed photographs.

She wasn't close enough to see who was in them, and now didn't seem like the time to wander over there.

Instead, she handed Eric the gift bag. "I have something for you."

He peered inside and removed the baby's picture. He studied it carefully, gauging it from every angle, the way an expectant father should. He even traced the image behind the glass.

Finally he said, "It looks more like a kidney bean than a peapod."

"I know. That's what I thought, too. But I'm not calling it Sweet Bean."

He cocked a half smile. "I like Sweet Bean."

"No way." She stifled a laugh, just as she'd done when she'd first seen the baby on the sonogram monitor. "It will never live that down. Besides, Sweet Pea was its original name."

"In the old Native way, names are easily changed. And Sweet Bean isn't something to live down. It's who he or she is right now. Later, it will become something else." He followed the outline of the fetus again. "It won't always be a bean."

How could she argue with his gentle enthusiasm? Supporting his decision, she said, "Sweet Bean it is. Until it becomes something else."

He carried the picture over to the fireplace mantel and placed it among the photos that were already there.

She followed him, pleased that he was giving their baby what appeared to be a place of honor. She was also curious to see the other pictures since she'd already wondered about them.

Most of them were of Kaley throughout the years,

starting in childhood and up to what she looked like now. She was an adorable kid and a lovely adult.

The only picture of Eric was from his wedding, on the beach with his bride in his arms. He was young and dashing and looked madly happy, the way Dana would have imagined him. Corrine appeared just as happy. She was lithe and tanned, draped in satin and lace, with her veil billowing joyfully in the breeze.

"You were a beautiful couple," she said.

"Thank you. It was one of the best days of my life. Along with the day we adopted Kaley."

And here he was, all these years later, having a baby with someone he barely knew. But Dana couldn't alter what was. She couldn't bring Corrine back or arrange it so that Sweet Bean had never been conceived. All she could do was move forward and try to make a go of things.

"Eric?"

"Yes?"

She turned away from his wedding photo, not wanting to look at it when she said this. "I made a decision."

He turned away from it, too. "About my proposal?"

"I'm going to accept, if the offer is still on the table."

He didn't respond right away, and she wondered if he was going to ask her to reconsider, to take more time to be absolutely certain. But then he softly said, "Of course it's still on the table." He finished his statement by adding, "I'm glad you're going to marry me. And I meant what I said about doing whatever I can to make it work. I'm going to try to be the best husband I can be to you and the best father I can be to our baby."

"Thank you. That means a lot to me."

He reached forward, and they embraced. She put her head on his shoulder and clutched his shirt.

Holding on for dear life.

Chapter Six

Eric felt as if he were having an out-of-body experience, holding the woman he was going to marry and feeling her heart beating against his.

When they separated, a stream of silence engulfed them, the moment turning intimately quiet. They stared at each other, the gravity of their engagement bouncing between them.

Because he didn't know how to cope with the tender feelings she incited, he steered the conversation in a practical direction. "At least now we don't have to worry about the medical stuff. Once we're married, I can put you on my health insurance."

"That's good." She seemed relieved that he'd broken the ice. "It will save me the trouble of looking for another policy." She fussed with the scarf/belt thing she was wearing, twisting the ends of the printed fabric. "It will probably save you money, too, from having to pay more than necessary."

He nodded, grateful that they both were making an effort to talk. It was certainly better than standing here in silence. Keeping the discussion going, he said, "When should we set the date?"

"If it's all right with you, I'd like to get married as soon as we can arrange it. It will make me too nervous to drag it out. But mostly I don't want to be showing when we take the plunge."

"What about the rings? Should we shop for those soon?" He glanced at his left hand where his ring used to be. He'd removed it soon after Corrine had died. It had been easier than strangers thinking he was still married. He returned his gaze to Dana. "I'd prefer to have a plain band. That's what I wore last time. But I can get you something fancy if you want." He'd given Corrine a diamond and it didn't seem fair not to give Dana one, too.

"Fancy rings are expensive, Eric."

"I can make payments on it."

"I don't think you should do that. Not with everything else we have going on. A plain gold band is fine for me, too. We can even shop online for a good deal."

The internet barely existed the first time he'd gotten married. He remembered walking into a jewelry store to buy the rings he and Corrine had chosen. It had been a major part of the engagement process.

She said, "We should probably keep the wedding itself simple, too. Of course there is a lot to consider. Where we should have it, who we should invite, the type of food we should serve, the cake, our wardrobe. I've already been thinking about a dress. Something just a little wild." She smiled. "The bohemian bride. Remember when you called me that?"

He smiled, too. He definitely remembered. "You can go as plain or wild as you want. Not just with your ring or your dress, but with everything. You can arrange the entire thing."

She tilted her head. "You're not going to be part of the planning?"

"I'd just cramp your style." He preferred for it to be her vision. Besides, he was too overwhelmed to tackle the details.

"It's going to be a lot of work on my own."

Was she trying to coax him into being part of it? Or was she just concerned about getting everything done in time? Either way, he thought of a solution. "I can ask Kaley if she can come over to meet you, maybe sometime next weekend. Then while she's here, she can help you plan it."

"That's a great idea. I'd love to have her help."

"I'm sure she'll make herself available whenever you need her."

"What are you going to do while your daughter and I are figuring out the arrangements?"

"I'll sit off to the sidelines and listen." And try to keep from floating into space.

"I'll do some wedding-planning research ahead of time so I'm prepared when I meet Kaley. What a first meeting, huh?"

"You won't be at a loss for things to talk about." He knew how much work went into a wedding.

"No doubt we'll be jabbering away."

"That's what girls usually do." And his daughter and his future bride were close enough in age to relate to each other. Eric was the odd guy out. Or more like the *old* guy out. He wasn't ancient, but compared to Dana and Kaley, he might as well be.

Dana said, "I'll do my best to keep it simple and cost-efficient, with just family and a few friends."

"As long as you make it nice for yourself."

"And for you, too."

"I'm sure you'll make it nice for both of us."

"Do you want to shop for the rings now?" she asked. "I think it would be fun to get started."

"Sure. I'll get my laptop." And make their engagement official.

On Sunday, Kaley flitted around Eric's kitchen, making a tray of finger sandwiches that she paired with store-bought salads and snacks. Eric watched her as she prepared to play hostess. She seemed nervous about meeting Dana.

"I wish I was a better cook," she said. "I wish I could make a special lunch for all of us."

"You baked cupcakes and cookies last summer."

"Because Victoria helped me. I never could have done that on my own. Does Dana cook?"

He thought about the big, hearty breakfast she'd served him on their morning-after. "Yes."

"As well as Victoria?"

"As far as I can tell." He'd even given Dana wifely points for her culinary skills.

"And as good as Mom, too."

"Again, as far as I can tell. I've only had a couple meals that Victoria fixed and only one that Dana made. Your mom cooked for me all the time."

"I'm glad Dana is young. I think it will make her

seem less like a stepmom and more like a friend. I don't need another mother. I had Mom and I have Victoria. Besides, if Dana was your age, you two probably wouldn't be having a baby. A woman in her forties probably wouldn't have gotten pregnant that easily."

Dana certainly conceived easily. One time. One expired condom. Eric's head was still reeling with it.

The doorbell chimed, and Kaley made a little leap into the air. "She's here." She pushed him out of the kitchen. "Go get the door."

"I'm going." He glanced back to see his daughter placing the sandwich platter on the table just so. When he opened the door, he couldn't help noticing how cute Dana looked. She was wearing her hair in a mass of blond waves, with one of her signature silk flowers clipped at her ear.

"That's pretty," he said.

"It's a plumeria blossom, like they wear in Hawaii." She touched the white-and-yellow ornament. "It's on my left side. See?"

Yes, he saw. When they first discussed the flowers she routinely wore, she'd told him the right side meant a woman was single and the left side implied that she was taken.

Should he lean forward and kiss her? Should he acknowledge that she belonged to him? Yes, he should. Not only was it a groom-type thing to do, he wanted to taste the sweetness of her lips. But because he couldn't quite pull it off, he merely stated the obvious. "You're taken now."

"I'm also pregnant and—" she removed her slip-on shoes and laughed "—barefoot."

He shook his head, smiled, wondered how a serious

man like himself was going to fare as her husband. He really should have kissed her, but the moment had already passed. "You're a nut, Dana."

"I try." She put her shoes back on and gazed past him.

He realized that Kaley must be standing there. He turned around. Sure enough, she was waiting to meet Dana.

The girls introduced themselves. They even went right for a hug. Kaley put her hand on Dana's stomach, too.

"I'm so excited about the baby," his daughter said. "I love the ultrasound picture you framed. It does look like a bean."

"Sweet Bean. Your dad had to convince me that name was okay."

"It is. It's perfect. Which reminds me, I have a gift for you. Hold on, and I'll go get it." Kaley made a mad dash for her room and came back with a teddy bear. "It's a Beanie Baby." She squished it to showcase the beans that were inside it. "I always thought these were cool because the manufacturer gives them birthdays. This one's is the same day as when the baby will be due. I went online and used a due date calculator to figure it out."

"Oh, my goodness. What a special gift. Thank you." Dana clutched the bear. "A Beanie Baby for Sweet Bean and with a proposed birthday that matches."

"When is the date?" Eric inquired. He was the father, yet he still didn't know. Like an idiot, he kept forgetting to ask.

"November nineteenth," came the simultaneous reply from Dana and Kaley. With a mutual laugh, they said, "Jinx," afterward.

Obviously they were getting along wonderfully, and they'd known each other all of a few minutes.

"Can I see the bear?" he asked.

Dana gave it to him, and he held the little toy in the palm of his hand. In November, he would be cradling his newborn son or daughter. God, he was scared.

He knew what raising a child entailed: the love, the exhaustion, the tears, the smiles, the laughter, Santa Claus, the Easter Bunny, the loss of a first tooth, excruciating bouts of the flu, arguments about eating too much junk food and not doing enough homework, laundry that needed washing, handing over the key to your car, prom night, college entrance exams.

He'd been through it all and now he would be going through it again. Was it any wonder he was scared?

He glanced at his grown daughter, but she wasn't paying any attention to him. Her focus was on Dana, and rightly so.

"Are you hungry?" Kaley asked the pregnant mom. "I made some finger sandwiches. I got some other stuff, too."

"That sounds great. I'm always hungry. I didn't used to be, but I am now. Eating helps me from getting queasy."

The three of them went into the dining room. Eric was still holding the bear.

He didn't sit at the table. He made up a plate for himself and took it into the living room. Although he could see and hear what was going on, his involvement would be indirect, the way he preferred it.

He put the bear on the coffee table, and one of his tabbies came out from under the couch to inspect it.

"So you do have cats," Dana said, from her vantage

point in the dining room. "Candy asked me if I thought you were a dog or cat person. I guessed cats."

"We have two," Kaley supplied, before Eric could respond. "They're brother and sister, from the same litter. Dad calls them the bougainvillea babies because when they were kittens, they used to hide in the bougainvillea on the patio."

Dana said, "Oh, that's funny. Bougainvillea babies, a Beanie Baby, and a Sweet Bean baby in my belly. We're besieged by babies."

The tabby swatted the teddy bear, then climbed onto Eric's lap while he ate his food. "For the record, I like dogs, too."

"Candy will be glad to hear that. She teaches doga. It's yoga for dogs. She teaches regular yoga, too. Candy is my landlord and my closet friend," she explained to Kaley. "When I told her we were going to start making wedding plans, she offered to let us use her place for the ceremony and reception. She suggested it because I want to get married in a setting surrounded by flowers, and she has the most beautiful garden in her yard. My side of the yard has a lovely garden, too." Dana hesitated, then asked Eric, "Would that location be okay with you?"

"Yes, of course. It's fine." The profusion of flowers definitely fit her. Plus the fountain she adored was there, too.

"Oh, good. Then that's where we'll have it." She turned to Kaley. "We can use my little house in the back as the bridal room, where the women in the ceremony can get ready. I want you and Candy to be my bridesmaids."

"Thank you. That's nice. I'd love to be one of your bridesmaids. What date are you aiming for?"

Dana recited a date that was about a month away and removed a sheet of paper from her purse. "I printed a checklist from the net about how to plan a wedding in thirty days."

"This is going to be so much fun." Kaley got girlish and giddy. "Can I see it?"

Dana handed over the list and Kaley read the instructions aloud. "Step one is to decide on the location. Yea! That's already done." She waited a chipper beat. "Step two is to compile the guest list and prepare the invitations, mailing them as soon as possible. Hmm. We better get cracking on that." Another quick pause. "Step three is getting your paperwork in order, like the marriage license. It says this should be done by day five." She shot Eric a glance. "Better look into that, Dad."

He lifted his brows. His bossy kid had taken it upon herself to delegate responsibility. But he noticed that Dana didn't seem to mind. If anything, she looked pleased to have such competent help.

Kaley spoke again. "Step four is to find a pastor or whoever you're going to use to deliver the vows. This is when you should hire a photographer, too, and start looking at rings."

"We've already got that covered," Dana said. "We ordered the rings on the day I accepted your dad's proposal. So we can cross that off the list."

Kaley made a happy checkmark in the air and forged ahead. "Step five is to choose the wedding party and decide on bridesmaids' dresses. Then they say to rent the groom's tux and purchase the bride's dress. If it was me, I'd look for a dress sooner than step five."

Dana responded, "Oh, believe me, I plan to. I'm going to shop at vintage stores."

"Really? I love thrifting."

"You can shop with me, if you'd like. Maybe we can find vintage bridesmaids dresses, too. Candy can shop with us so we can decide together."

"This is so cool." Kaley bounced in her seat, took a breath and continued. "The final steps are ordering the cake, arranging the food for the reception and paying for the flowers. Of course all of this is supposed to be done simply. You can't get frilly flowers or a custom-made cake in that short amount of time."

Dana remarked, "I intend to keep everything simple, but I want it to be pretty, too."

"It will be," Kaley assured her. "We can even make our own decorations. That will keep the cost down, but still give you the kind of pretty you want."

Eric remained quiet. But even so, he was glad that Kaley and Dana were thriving on the festivities.

He asked Dana, "Have you told your family about us?"

"Oh, yes, I finally did, and they're thrilled that I'm going to be a married mom."

"Are they concerned about our age difference?"

"Not at all. In fact, they think me being married to someone in his forties will be good for me. That it will help settle me down."

Apparently Eric was the only one who thought the difference was an issue. "I can't imagine me taming you."

Kaley chimed in. "It will probably be more like her pepping you up. I love you more than anyone, Dad. But sometimes you can be a downer."

"Gee, thanks. Can we change the subject now?" He didn't want to talk about what a downer he was.

Dana changed it. "Have you told your family?" she asked him.

"Kaley is my family. My parents are gone, and I was an only child. I don't have any extended family to speak of."

"Besides Ryan and Victoria," Kaley said, reminding him of her birth parents.

"Yes," he agreed. "They've become like a brother and sister to me. I'm going to ask Ryan to be my best man." Just as Eric would be Ryan's best man.

"Isn't it crazy?" Kaley remarked. "That you're getting married before them? Who ever thought that would happen?"

Not him, that was for sure.

"Are Ryan and Victoria planning to have more children?" Dana asked.

"Not for a while," Eric replied. "Our baby is going to be the only baby for a few years, at least."

"My first brother or sister." Kaley smiled, then reached for a pen and paper. "Who else do you plan to invite to the wedding, Dad, besides Ryan and Victoria?"

"A few coworkers and some of my powwow and artist friends." He didn't socialize much these days. His list would be small. He also needed to hurry up and tell people that he was getting married before the invitations went out. Just one more thing to be nervous about, he thought.

He glanced at Dana. She didn't seem nervous. She'd slipped easily into bride mode. The afternoon continued with further wedding discussion, then ended with

Dana and Kaley hugging goodbye and promising to get back in touch to arrange a shopping day.

Eric did his part, offering to pay for everything associated with the ceremony, including the wardrobe and decorations. Dana thanked him with a smile.

When the time came, he returned the Beanie Baby to her and walked her out to her car.

"I adore your daughter," she said, as they stood at the curb. "She's amazing."

"She obviously thinks you're amazing, too."

"It helps that I'm going to be the mother of her brother or sister."

"Family is everything to her. But she would have been impressed with you, anyway. You're easy to like."

"So are you."

"I used to be easier to like." He couldn't blame Kaley for calling him a downer, even if it hurt to hear it.

"I think you're doing great, Eric."

Not as great as she was. She was charming and optimistic and everything he wasn't. "I'm not doing as well as you are."

"You're doing the best you can. That's all that matters."

Could she be any more understanding? "You're going to be a hell of a wife, Dana."

She flashed a dazzling smile and cocked both hands on her hips. "So I'm going to be more than just scattered and messy?"

"Yeah. A lot more." She was already proving to be a good partner. He reached for the flower at her ear and gave it an affectionate tug.

Finally, he leaned forward and kissed her. But it was brief and chaste, considering that they were standing in front of his house in the middle of the day. Still, it felt good to taste what he'd been missing.

Making Eric long for her touch even after she was gone.

The following day, Eric called Ryan. After the usual exchange of greetings, he got right to the point. "I know this is going to come as a shock, but I'm getting married in a month and I wanted to ask you to be my best man."

"Wow. Married? You're right. That is a shock, but it's wonderful, too. Of course I'll be your best man. It would be my honor. Who's the lucky lady you fell in love with?"

Eric replied with honesty, with the kind of blatancy that made his stomach tense. "I'm not in love with her, and she isn't in love with me. She's pregnant and we're making a go of it for the baby."

Stalled silence. Then, "Are you sure that's the right thing to do?"

"I think so. It's the best way for me to be in the baby's life and provide the support Dana needs."

"Dana? Is that your bride's name?"

"Yes." To make sure Ryan understood how important it was to her, he relayed her family history.

"I can see how that complicates things, but can't you wait a while to be sure it's what you should do?"

"She wants to have the ceremony before she starts showing. Besides, what difference will a few more months make? I offered to marry her before the baby comes, and that's what I'm going to do. Kaley and Dana are already planning the wedding."

"I guess it's safe to assume that Dana and Kaley are friends."

"They hit it off beautifully and they only met for the first time last night."

"Damn. What a whirlwind."

"It definitely is. Dana and I only had one date, one night together. We hardly know each other." The more he revealed, the crazier it sounded. "She's younger than me, too. I was leery of dating her because of the age difference."

"And now you're marrying her? You're not stating a very strong case for yourself. Maybe you should postpone it."

"I'm not backing out." He could never do that to Dana or the baby. Nor did he want to. "Dana is going to make a really good wife and mother. I'm the one who needs to work on being prepared."

"That's just my point. My first marriage didn't work, as you well know."

Yes, Eric knew that Ryan was divorced, but it wasn't the same scenario. "You didn't marry her for the sake of a child." Ryan didn't have children with his ex.

"I married her because I loved her. But I didn't love her enough for the marriage to thrive. Victoria was always there, taking up space in my heart."

The way Corrine's memory filled Eric's heart. "I'm not a teenager like you were when Victoria got pregnant. I'm a grown man, and I'm fortunate enough to be able to marry the mother of my child."

"A woman you don't love."

"She's a wonderful person. Beautiful and smart and funny. So just wish me well and stop trying to persuade me to rethink my decision."

"Of course I wish you well. I want the best for you

and Dana and the baby. And for Kaley. I can only imagine how excited she is about being a big sister."

"She's over the moon. She thinks Dana and I are meant to be."

"As they say, God works in mysterious ways. You and Corrine couldn't conceive, and now a woman comes along who gets pregnant from one date. Maybe this *is* meant to be."

"Now you sound like Kaley."

"You just told me to be supportive."

"You're right, I did. I'm sorry if I'm not making any sense." Eric shook his head at his own confusion. "It's just weird. Me having a kid at this age."

"You're an incredible father to Kaley and you'll be an incredible dad to this one."

"I already have a picture of it. Dana gave me a copy of the ultrasound photo."

"You can show it me to when Victoria and I come for the wedding. She's going to be as surprised as I was to hear your news."

"I'll be in touch with the details. And thanks, Ryan, for agreeing to stand up for me. It'll be good to have you there."

"It'll be good to be there. We'll talk again soon. Give Kaley our love."

"I always do." They said goodbye and hung up, leaving Eric as anxious as ever.

Confiding in Ryan hadn't been enough to calm his nerves. He needed to talk to Corrine, too.

Chapter Seven

Eric drove to the florist located at the cemetery. He always got Corrine's flowers at that same shop. It was easier since everyone else was also buying gifts for the dead. He didn't have to explain what the occasion was or cross paths with anyone except mourners. Plus, by now, the shopkeeper knew him.

After he chose the bouquet he wanted, he walked to his wife's grave, taking a long, tree-lined path, flanked by mounds of grass and rows of headstones.

He knelt in front of her marker and put the flowers in place. "I got you orchids," he said. "The kind you carried on our wedding day." The same type he'd given Dana on their first date. "You wouldn't believe everything that's been going on."

This wasn't like the conversation he'd had with Ryan. No one was on the other side, reacting to his words. But he'd been conversing with Corrine this way for a while now, and it had begun to seem natural.

"I have a lot to tell you," he said. The last time he'd had this much to say was when Kaley had found her birth parents. But this was different. This was about Dana.

"Remember the waitress who gave me the rose that I brought to you? I'm going to marry her, Corrine. She asked me on a date and I spent the night with her and now she's pregnant."

He rearranged the orchids. "You probably think this is going to be good for me. Kaley thinks so, too. She doesn't know about the discussion you and I had before you died, but she seems to know that you would approve, anyway. As soon as I told her about the baby, she insisted that I marry Dana. It's important to Dana, too, because she comes from a line of unwed mothers and she wants our child to be legitimate. I wish I could say that I'm excited about getting married again, but I feel like a passenger on a runaway train. It's all happening so fast, and I don't know if I'm going to be any good at it.

"I talked to Ryan about it earlier and asked him to be my best man. After I told him how I felt, he tried to discourage me from getting married so soon. But I have to do what's right for Dana and the baby, even if I'm nervous about it…" He paused, blew out his breath. "That makes sense, doesn't it?"

Naturally, he didn't get a response. There was nothing but a stone marker and his own rambling words.

"Kaley thinks it's fate. She thinks it's meant to be. She's thrilled about the baby. She and Dana are getting along great, too. They're planning the wedding together."

Again, he was met with silence.

He kept talking. "I'm scared about becoming a new father. I was young and hopeful when we adopted Kaley. It's not the same this time. We gave the baby a cute nickname, though." He couldn't help but smile. "Sweet Bean. Dana framed the ultrasound picture for me, and I put it on the mantel." He stopped smiling. "It's sitting there, next to our wedding photo. What am I supposed to do with that picture now, Corrine? I can't leave it on the mantel after Dana and I get married. That wouldn't be fair to her. But it's going to feel strange to remove it. I'm so confused about how to have a new wife and a new child. Dana is handling everything much better than I am. But life hasn't beaten her up the way it has with me. She's never been in love or lost the person she loved."

He plucked mindlessly at a blade of grass.

"The good thing, though, is that she understands what I had with you. I've been able to talk to her about it. She's a pretty amazing girl, sweet and understanding.

"The problem is me. I'm concerned that I won't be able to live up to my promise. I'm going to try to make her happy, but what if I fall short? What if I can't pull it off?"

Eric glanced up at the heavens and noticed how closely the sky mirrored the color of Dana's eyes. "How weird is that?" he said to Corrine. "Your eyes were blue, too, but today I see hers. Do you think that's a good sign?" Surely, it must be. Dana was alive and Corrine was gone.

He stopped looking at the sky. Even if it was a positive omen, he was still worried about fulfilling his up-coming vows.

He stood up, preparing to go home. He couldn't stay here forever. "I'll see you next time," he said. He would be back to visit Corrine, as always. But for now he needed to get a grip on becoming Dana's husband.

The ceremony was officially two weeks away, and Dana was grateful for Kaley's and Candy's help.

Today they were shopping—again—for the dresses, hers included. They hadn't found anything on their previous excursions, but they were going to more stores this time.

The wedding colors would be determined by the dresses that Kaley and Candy chose. Dana didn't mind leaving it to chance. She trusted their judgment, whether they chose matching garments or two separate styles. It didn't matter, as long as everyone felt good in what they were wearing.

By one in the afternoon, Candy found her prize: a turquoise-colored granny dress from the early 1970s, with an embroidered neckline.

That set Kaley in motion, looking for a seventies granny dress, too. She squealed when she uncovered a yellow one with a similar neckline that looked incredible on her.

There it was. The colors were turquoise and yellow, a super combination. Dana couldn't have been more pleased. Her bridesmaids were going to be bright and beautiful.

"Your turn," Candy said to Dana. "We have to find the perfect dress for you. This is going to be your day, after all."

Her day. Her new life. "I'll find the right one. I can feel it."

Two stores later, she zeroed in on a long white cocktail dress from the same era as the bridesmaids' dresses that could easily double as a wedding gown. She tried it on and sighed in delight. What she loved most were the tiny multicolored jewels sprinkled throughout the fabric to form daisy shapes. The gown had an ethereal quality, but at the same time, made a bold and free-spirited statement.

Candy and Kaley fussed over her, telling her how stunning she looked. She was definitely going to buy it. Not only did it fit her style, it was marvelously affordable.

"Are you going to wear a veil, a fancy comb, or a crown of flowers in your hair?" Eric's daughter asked. "Any of it would work."

"I don't know." The possibilities seemed endless.

"Let's get some lunch," Candy said. "Then we can go to bridal shops and check out the accessories."

While they ate, they chatted excitedly about the wedding. Dana was determined to maintain her sunny disposition and be her usual exuberant self, to make the most of marrying Eric, even if he was cautious about marrying her. She understood how scary this was for him. But for her it was becoming an adventure.

Of course this was the party-planning stage. Why wouldn't it be fun, especially with the bridesmaids sharing her enthusiasm?

After lunch, they continued shopping, hitting bridal shops, as Candy had suggested.

There were tons of lovely accessories. Dana tried on veils and headbands and an assortment of combs.

Then Kaley said, "Look over here," drawing her attention to another display case.

Immediately Dana knew why. On the second shelf were jeweled hairpins, in the shape of daisies, in every color imaginable. They were small and delicate and oh so perfect.

Candy peered into the case, too. "Oh, Dana. Those look as if they were designed just for your dress."

"I know. Can you believe it?"

"You could fix your hair so it's half up and half down," Kaley said. "And you could put those little pins all throughout, making them an intricate part of the design."

"What a fabulous idea. I'll get most of them in turquoise and yellow, so they'll tie in with the wedding colors. But I'll get some in other colors, too, like the daisies on my dress." She felt like Cinderella in the making. But that was how a bride should feel.

After she'd made the purchase, they agreed to go the craft store to look for things to use to make the centerpieces for the tables.

"I already conned Dad into helping us make the decorations," Kaley said.

"You did?" Dana hadn't expected him to get involved.

"He tried to refuse, but I made a stink about how he's an artist and how he should put his talent to use for us."

"Good thinking," Dana said. "We'll just get a bunch of interesting stuff and let him figure out how to make it work." She adored the thought of Eric's participation.

She wanted her groom to start enjoying the wedding in any way he could.

* * *

On the day Eric, Dana and Kaley were going to make the centerpieces, Kaley called and said she was running late and to get started without her.

Eric sat at one of the work tables in his studio, with Dana by his side. She'd arrived on time, so for now it was just the two of them, sorting through the craft items she'd brought with her.

He took inventory: silk daisies, turquoise and yellow ribbon in various widths and textures, plastic jewels in an array of colors, long white ostrich plums, acrylic champagne glasses, shiny gold candles and an assortment of glittery baskets.

"What do you think?" Dana asked.

What he thought was that they'd bought way more stuff than was necessary, but he'd agreed to work on this project so he was going to use his imagination and make it fly.

He asked, "How many centerpieces do we need?"

"Four. But we figured that we could use anything that's leftover to decorate the cake table."

"Then how about this? We can make each centerpiece different—one that's floral, another one showcasing the feathers, another one with the champagne glasses and the final one with the candles. That will give us the four we need, with plenty of items left over to create something for the cake table that uses all of the above."

"That sounds great." She flashed a feminine smile. "I thought about bringing over my dress so you could see it and use it for inspiration, but then I decided that it would be more exciting for you to see it the first time on our wedding day." She smiled again. "With me in it."

"I'm sure that you're going to look beautiful." He studied her, thinking how pretty she looked now, amid the shimmery craft decor. "You always do."

"Thank you."

"Before we get started, do you want to see your ring and try it on to make sure it fits? If not, we'll have to get it resized. I already tried mine, and it was fine."

"Yes, of course I want to try mine, too. I didn't know you had them."

"They came in yesterday."

Eric left the studio and got her ring. He returned and handed her the velvet-lined box.

She opened it and slipped on the ring. "It's a perfect fit." She moved her hand around, making the gold catch the light.

It did fit well, but that didn't change how plain and simple it was. She'd graciously agreed on an unadorned gold band to keep the cost down, but he still thought that she should have something fancier, especially now that he'd seen how lavishly she'd chosen to decorate for the wedding.

He glanced at the silk flowers. "What made you decide on daisies as part of the theme?"

"My dress has daisies on it."

"Maybe I should have a jeweler engrave some daisies on your ring." At least that would embellish it a bit.

Her eyes lit up. "Really? Oh, that would be wonderful. I'd like that."

When she removed the ring and handed it to him, he thought about an aspect of the wedding they'd yet to discuss. "As long as we're figuring things out, what do you want to do for the honeymoon?"

She seemed surprised. "We're going to have a honeymoon?"

"We won't be able to go away or anything like that. I can't get the time off from work. But we can take a few days and do something locally."

"How about the zoo?"

He didn't know what he'd expected her to say, but that wasn't it. "The zoo?"

She nodded. "It's one of my favorite places."

"Then we'll go there for sure. We'll walk around and eat ice cream and do what people do on those sorts of outings."

She smiled. "My ice cream is going to be chocolate."

He smiled, too. He knew what a chocolate freak she was. "Is there anything else that you want to do?"

"On our honeymoon? It would be nice for us to stay in a hotel." She nibbled her bottom lip and the uncharacteristic gesture made her seem shy and old-fashioned. "You know, so it feels more romantic."

His pulse started to pound. As strange as all of this was, there was no denying the chemistry between them. "Will you wear the cherry blossom perfume?"

"I'm wearing it right now."

Should he move closer? Should he bury his face against her neck and inhale her skin? Or should he keep the temptation at bay?

He chose to abstain. It seemed sexier that way. "I'm not going to kiss you again until we're married. I'm not going to do anything to you until then."

She chewed her lip a little harder. "Now I really want to be together that night."

So did he. But they didn't talk any more about it. Kaley arrived, and they worked on the centerpieces.

Even if their honeymoon was becoming a much-thought about distraction.

Eric called around and found a local jeweler to engrave Dana's ring. As he entered the store, a wave of anxiety swept through him. He hadn't been in a jewelry store since he and Corrine had chosen their rings, and the memory hit him hard and deep. Suddenly he wasn't comfortable doing this.

He didn't like walking in here, presenting himself as a groom. He didn't want to be congratulated. Nor did he want to answer sentimental questions about the wedding. He hoped the girl at the counter was indifferent to him and the daisies he would be requesting.

Unfortunately that wasn't the case. The vivacious brunette commended him for having the ring engraved with what she called "the perfect little flower."

"Did you know that daisies are the symbol of truth and innocence? They can mean pure of body, but they can also mean pure of mind, soul and heart. Maidens used to pick them to put them in their hair. Is your bride going to wear daisies in her hair?" she asked.

"I don't know." He found himself adding, "But she often wears flowers in her hair. She chose this type of flower for the wedding because her dress has daisies on it. I haven't seen the dress, though."

"Oh, I like that. You're sticking to tradition."

Eric couldn't believe that he was having this conversation with a stranger, doing exactly what he didn't want to do.

The salesgirl smiled big and wide. "Did you get her an engagement ring to go with the band?"

"No. We're keeping it simple."

"In case you want to shake things up, we actually have a ring that would go perfectly with—"

"No, that's okay."

"It's an Edwardian daisy cluster ring. We deal in antique jewelry, too."

Eric's curiosity was piqued. Dana loved vintage things. But he wasn't here to add another ring to the mix. Still, it made him stop and think. He'd wanted to get her something nicer from the beginning.

The brunette persisted. "It's already priced lower than most pieces from that era, but I'm sure I can get you an even better price if you're interested. It's lovely, I swear."

"Sure. Why not? I'd like to see it."

She darted over to another case and came back with the ring, which featured a series of natural cut diamonds in the shape of a single daisy.

Eric had to agree, it *was* lovely, bright and delicate. He noticed that it had a few flaws. But that didn't seem to matter. There was something uniquely charming about it, just the way it was.

"Wouldn't it look smashing with the gold band you're having engraved? What a creative bridal set they would make." To prove her point, she placed both of them on a velvet-covered ring display, showing him how beautifully they fit. "They could easily be soldered together. A lot of bridal sets are done that way."

He nodded. Corrine had done that with hers after they'd gotten married. But doing it beforehand made sense with this set since he would be placing both rings on Dana's finger at the ceremony.

Both rings? He hadn't committed to buy the Edwardian piece. He was only looking at it. But now that he'd seen it, he couldn't imagine walking out of the store without buying it. It just didn't seem right not to give Dana a bridal set that shined as brightly as her personality.

He studied the daisy. The perfect flower. For the imperfect marriage. The comparison made him frown.

"You don't like it?" the girl asked.

"No, I do. Very much."

"Is it the price? I meant what I said about getting you an even better deal."

He couldn't tell her what was wrong. "Everything is fine. I'd like to negotiate on it."

She called the owner over, and they agreed on an acceptable price. The owner promised to engrave the gold band, size the antique ring and solder them together in plenty of time for the wedding. He decided that he was going to keep it a secret from Dana, surprising her with it on that day.

And although he was feeling good about his purchase, the feeling didn't last. He went home, a soon-to-be groom, nervous once again.

Chapter Eight

This was it. The big day. The wedding.

Dana stood in front of a full-length mirror in her bedroom, with her mother and grandmother by her side. Kaley and Candy were there, too.

"You make a stunning bride," Grandma said, tears welling in her eyes. Mom was teary-eyed, as well.

They'd arrived two days ago and were staying with Dana in her little house. But tonight that was going to change. After the wedding, Dana would be honeymooning in a hotel with her new husband, then moving into his house to make a life with him.

She gazed at Mom and Grandma in the mirror, where their reflections shimmered next to hers. Mom was in a silvery blue dress, and Grandma wore shades of pink. Grandma's hair was white, and Mom's was blond, with slight threads of gray. Although she was only fifty, she looked and seemed much older. Dana couldn't remember a time when Mom seemed or acted young. Of course there had been that one reckless night when Dana had been conceived, proof that Mom had been young once.

She smiled at both women in the mirror. Thankfully she was making them happy by marrying the father of her child.

In the silence that followed, she touched her still-flat stomach. Soon she would reach the twelve-week mark, which she heard was the magic number that would most likely end her morning sickness. She was definitely looking forward to that.

"We better take our seats," Grandma said. "And let you girls prepare to walk down the aisle."

Mom took Dana's hand and squeezed it. "Before we go, I want to tell you how much I like Eric."

"He likes you, too." He'd already told Dana how nice and kind her family was.

"I made him promise to take good care of you."

"Oh, Mom." Could she be any more archaic? "I don't need anyone to take care of me."

"I think you do. So I wanted him to make that promise. And he did. Very sincerely, I might add."

Because Eric was archaic, too. Otherwise he wouldn't be forcing himself to marry her. Dana knew how difficult it was for him, certainly harder for him than it was for her. She was approaching their marriage with gusto. If she didn't, she would worry her fool head off, and she was determined to remain strong and happy, no matter what.

Her mom said, "He did seem a bit nervous, waiting around for the ceremony to happen, but most grooms are. I can't fault him for that."

And neither could Dana. Eric was a good man with good intentions.

Mom and Grandma went outside, and Dana turned to Kaley and Candy. Her bridesmaids were as beautiful as she knew they would be. They thought she was beautiful, too.

"You look like a princess," Kaley said to her. "With flowers, lace and shiny jewels."

"I agree." Candy handed Dana the bridal bouquet, which was a glorious ensemble of white daisies, wrapped in turquoise and yellow ribbon.

Then Kaley said, "I'm so glad that you're going to be part of my family."

"So am I." She embraced Eric's daughter and held tight. "Have you seen your dad today?"

"Yes, and he's more nervous than I've ever seen him. He didn't tell me he was, but I can tell."

"My mom mentioned that he seemed nervous. I'm a little nervous, too."

"Don't be. You're the most beautiful bride ever."

Dana blew out the breath in her lungs. Her heart was pounding. "I just want to be a good wife."

"You will be."

"It's almost time," Candy interjected. She opened the door, listening for the "Wedding March" to begin.

Dana's heart pounded even more.

As soon as the music started, the bridesmaids grabbed their bouquets, told her how beautiful she was one last time and left together. Dana waited by herself. She didn't have a father, or anyone equivalent, available to take her arm and walk her down the aisle.

The moment came, and she stepped into the garden, where the makeshift aisle and altar had been created.

As she made her way down the floral-lined path, she caught sight of her groom, standing tall and straight. He'd already turned to face her.

He looked incredible, clothed in a classic black tuxedo, with the sun shining behind him. She could tell that he approved of the way she looked, too. Their attraction to each other was palpable.

As she continued her approach, she noticed the guests, eclectic group that they were, watching her. She suspected that Mom and Grandma were crying.

Once Dana reached the altar, she met Eric's gaze. Overwhelmed by his masculine beauty, by the wedding itself, she smiled at him. Although he returned her smile, it didn't register in his eyes. She wanted to make him smile for real. Even if their marriage didn't last, she wanted to make Eric happy, for as long as possible.

The bride wanted to fix the groom? That wasn't supposed to be part of the deal. But deep down, she knew it was. She couldn't be married to a broken man without trying to repair him.

The justice of the peace they hired to officiate was a white-haired man with a twinkle in the corners of his eyes. He reminded Dana of the old wizard who ruled Oz. He conducted the ceremony with pride, obviously enjoying his role in the wedding.

It went as planned until the rings were exchanged. The gold band that Eric put on her finger wasn't the one she'd been expecting. It was a bridal set, with a magnificent diamond daisy attached.

She gasped, then glanced up at him. His lips curved into a genuine smile. He was happy that he'd surprised her. It didn't necessarily mean they'd have lifelong happiness, but it was a wondrous start.

Tears rushed to Dana's eyes. She was anxious for the part in the ceremony where they were supposed to kiss.

The vows were short and to the point, maybe even a little choppy. Eric was no longer smiling. She reminded herself of how nervous he was.

Soon the kiss happened, but it seemed rushed, too. But only because it felt so good to have his lips pressed softly against hers. It made her want more. She even thought about the honeymoon and imagined how glorious it was going to be.

After that, Eric and Dana were pronounced husband and wife by the wizard who'd married them.

In the next breathless moment, Dana gazed at her groom. He was looking at her, too. Then they turned and faced their guests, who applauded them with cheer. Dana felt very much like a bride and she loved the feeling. Even Eric was smiling again.

During the reception, she paid special attention to Kaley's birth parents—as they were the guests who mattered most to Eric.

Ryan and Victoria made a stunning couple. Both in their mid-thirties, they embodied love and commitment. They exchanged tender glances. They exuded strength and confidence in their relationship. Clearly, they were meant to be together.

Ryan possessed dark hair, dark eyes and a country-boy smile. Victoria was fair-skinned with sleek red hair and ladylike warmth. Kaley had inherited their best qualities.

Dana couldn't help but envy them. She was certain that their life together would be flawless.

She glanced over at Eric. He was mingling with her family, being the proper groom. But he had little choice, she supposed. Mom and Grandma hadn't quit fussing over him. He'd even promised Grandma a dance. But first he would be dancing with Dana.

The playlist ranged from Tony Bennett to the Beatles to Beyoncé, and just about everything you could think of in between.

The first song, however, was Louis Armstrong's "What a Wonderful World." Dana had chosen it because she wanted everything in the world she and Eric would be creating to be wonderful.

The groom took her in his arms, and they danced. He was an exceptional dancer, and he looked the part, too. Classy. Debonair. Dana wondered what it would be like to fall in love with him.

Oh, no, she thought. She shouldn't be fantasizing about—

About what? Falling in love with the man she'd just married? Of course she should. It would be ludicrous *not* to have those types of fantasies. He was hot as sin, and she was having his baby. That was a damned good combination.

"I like what you did with your hair," he said, as they swayed to the song.

"Thank you. The style was Kaley's idea."

"Will you let me take it down tonight and remove all of those little pins?"

Her skin tingled. Tonight. At the hotel. "Yes, of course."

"The girl who sold me your ring told me that maidens used to pick daisies and wear them in their hair. She said that they're considered the perfect little flower."

"I love my ring. Thank you so much for giving it to

me. It's more than I could ever ask for, and I love how you made a bridal set out of it."

"That was the salesgirl's suggestion. The engagement ring is from the Edwardian era. It seemed right for you, given how you're into vintage things."

"It was wonderful of you to think of me." Wonderful. Like the song she'd picked. Wonderful. The way life should be.

"I don't like that everyone else is watching us," he said.

"You're doing fine, Eric. You're getting through it."

"So are you. But in a perfect world, you would've married a man you love. Not some broken-down guy like me."

Even he was calling himself broken. "I married you because I'm having your baby." Besides, she'd already been engrossed in bridal fantasies about falling in love with him. Surely that counted for something.

"How has Sweet Bean been treating you?"

"Fine. Except for the morning sickness."

He made a sorry face. "Bad baby. Making its mommy toss her cookies."

She laughed. "Now that's a romantic visual."

Much to her delight, he laughed, too, and she adored the way it transformed him.

When the song ended, he said, "You're wearing the cherry perfume blossom perfume like I wanted you to."

"I wasn't sure if you noticed."

"I definitely did."

She got another case of the tingles. Slow and sweet and sexy. "Our cake has cherry filling."

"It does? Damn."

"I ordered it just for you," she teased him. "I'll feed you some later, the way I'm supposed to."

"With everyone watching? Can't we save the cake for the honeymoon? To go along with the cherry treat I arranged?"

"You arranged a cherry treat?"

"For when we're alone."

She assumed it had something to with the honeymoon. The slow, sweet and sexy feeling quickened.

They danced to a few more songs, then separated and danced with other people. But she watched him from the corner of her eye. This man she'd just married. He was dancing with her grandmother, as promised, and Grandma looked young and refreshed in his arms.

After that, he danced with his daughter. That prompted Ryan to ask Dana to dance, which felt a little weird at first. Was Kaley's birth father sizing her up? Deciding if she was right for Eric?

"Kaley is crazy about you," he said.

She relaxed. "I'm crazy about her, too."

They both glanced in her direction. She was still dancing with Eric.

Dana said, "She helped me organize the wedding. I couldn't have done this without her and Candy."

"It's a very nice wedding. You all did a remarkable job."

"Thank you. It's been great to meet you and Victoria."

"Did Eric tell you that I was jealous of him when we first met?"

"No. He never mentioned that."

"I manifested this whole ridiculous scenario in my mind that he was going to be the man in Victoria's life instead of me. That they would fall in love and I would never have her. But they were just friends. There was never anything between them."

Dana appreciated his candor and the way he was opening up to her. "Thank you for sharing that with me. I still don't know that much about Eric."

"You'll learn as you go."

She kept quiet. She didn't have the courage to admit that she'd been wondering what loving Eric would be like. She wasn't going to tell anyone about those fantasies, except maybe Candy.

Finally she said, "He's still hurting over Corrine."

"He went through a lot with her. The way her sickness lingered. The hope that she would survive. The despair when she didn't."

"Do you know where she's buried?"

"No. But I know that Eric visits her grave as often as he can. Kaley goes there, too, but not as much as he does."

"Eric has never said anything about how Corrine's passing affected Kaley. She's never discussed it with me, either."

"She talked to me and Victoria about it when we all first spent time together. It affected her as terribly as it affected Eric, but she's gotten stronger as time has gone on. I guess kids really are more resilient. I lost my mom when I was young, too."

"I'm sorry."

"Mostly I was too young to remember her, but not having a mom was tough. My dad raised me by himself. He died a few years back. We had a strained relationship, but I loved him."

"I've never met my dad. I didn't know anything

about him, except his first name. But Eric probably already told you my family history."

"Yes, he did. And I understand. Fathers can sometimes be elusive. I certainly was." He frowned. "What I did to Victoria when Kaley was born was wrong."

"I'm glad it worked out for all of you."

"So am I."

She pondered what he'd said about himself. "It's interesting that you used the word *elusive*. That's exactly how I think of my father. Only he didn't do anything wrong because he doesn't know I exist. Of course if he did, he might have walked away. It's impossible to know how it would have turned out."

"Your baby is going to have a good father." He smiled. "And a good mother, too."

Touched by his words, she smiled, as well. "Thank you."

They parted ways, with what appeared to be friendship brewing between them. Dana was going to make a point of trying to get to know Victoria on a deeper level, too. Maybe not here and now, but when the moment presented itself.

The festivities continued, with an announcement that it was time to cut the cake. Dana shot Eric a come-hither look. He shook his head and approached the cake table with her.

"Behave," he whispered.

"Me?" she whispered back. "I'm as innocent as the night you made me pregnant."

He raised his eyebrows. Apparently her message was clear. She'd seduced him that night, just as she was seducing him now.

Together they reached for the ribbon-wrapped knife.

The cake was lovely, with white cream frosting and sugared daisies.

They cut into it, and her heart pounded. She suspected that his was thumping, too. All eyes were on them.

"You're supposed to feed it to me first," she said.

"I know." He broke off a small piece, without the filling, and lifted it to her mouth. The portion he'd chosen had a daisy on it. He was very gentle, no cake smashing, but a bit of the frosting did get on her lips. She licked it away.

"It's yummy," she said. She used that word deliberately since it was a word she'd also used to describe Eric. She knew he caught the reference. She saw the recognition in his eyes.

He stared at her mouth, then wiped his hands on a napkin. Now it was her turn to feed him.

She broke off a bigger piece for him, coating her fingers with cherries and white fluff. She put it directly into his mouth. Though brides and grooms were notorious for animated cake feedings, she doubted that it seemed sensual to anyone else.

But she heard Eric's breath hitch as he tasted the treat. Obviously to him, her intention was clear.

"Good?" she asked.

He nodded and swallowed. Was he thinking about their upcoming honeymoon? The night they were going to spend alone in a big luxurious bed? She definitely was.

To seal the deal, she kissed him while he had frosting on his lips. That got a rise out of everyone. Lots of pictures were snapped. Eric reacted like a hungry groom and looped an arm around her waist, pulling her closer.

He was definitely thinking about the honeymoon. The kiss was quick and hot and wildly exciting. Dana was glad that she'd gotten him to misbehave with her.

After the ceremony wound down, the guests wished them well and said goodbye, leaving with little bags of wedding favors.

Dana's mother and grandmother had an early flight in the morning, but they promised that they would come back after the baby was born. For now, they were going to retire to Dana's house for the rest of the night.

Dana turned to her husband. The Town Car he'd hired was waiting to take them to the hotel. The driver put their bags in the trunk and they climbed into the backseat, still wearing their wedding attire. Dana didn't want to change because she wanted Eric to strip off her silky white gown. She suspected that he was looking forward to the disrobing, too. Sex was their comfort zone. The act they already knew they did well together.

And were anxious to do again.

Chapter Nine

As Eric and Dana entered the lobby, they were greeted with smiles and congratulatory greetings from strangers, as well as the hotel staff.

Since Eric been a groom before, he knew what to expect in this type of setting. But it still caused a bit of unease. It wasn't only the attention. It was another reminder of the commitment he'd made, the promise to love, honor and protect the woman he'd just married.

The honor and protect part was easy. But love? He didn't take that word lightly. He knew better than anyone what it entailed. Joy. Beauty. Pain.

He glanced over at Dana. She was standing next to him at the check-in desk, with a happy expression on her face. Unable to help himself, he reached out to touch her cheek. She was so vivacious and so damned sweet.

She kissed the palm of his hand, and he realized how

"in love" they probably looked to those around them. Funny, how easily things could be misperceived.

One thing was certain. Eric wanted to bed his new wife. He wanted to lose himself in the luxury of her body, to take of her freely.

She shot him a sultry smile, letting him know she was thinking of how freely she wanted to indulge in him, too. His zipper went unbearably tight. She'd already driven him crazy with the cake feeding, and now she was doing it again.

They finished checking in and took the elevator to their room.

"Are you going carry me across the threshold?" she asked, as they stood outside the door. She playfully added, "I suggest that you lift me while you can." She made a big belly motion in front of her, teasing him about her pregnancy.

Trust Dana to crack a joke. He laughed and scooped her up, glad that her humor was infectious.

She squealed and gave him a loud smacking kiss. "Exactly what the bride ordered."

"Now all I have to do is figure out how to get the door open." He struggled to balance her. "I think I should have unlocked the room first."

"No problem. I can help." She took the keycard from him. She even turned the handle, making it easier for him to carry her inside.

He went straight for the bedroom and tossed her on the bed. She hit the mattress with a delicate bounce.

"Check out this place," she said, looking all aflutter. "It's swanky."

Yeah, it was. He'd seen pictures of it online when he'd made the reservations. But he didn't care about the decor, at least not at the moment. His agenda was to get her naked.

Then he remembered the bellhop had yet to deliver their bags. Room service was supposed to be on its way with complimentary goodies, too.

"Is this a honeymoon suite?" she asked.

"It's not a honeymoon suite, per se. This hotel doesn't have those. Instead they offer honeymoon and romance packages, which includes this type of accommodations."

"What else does the package include?"

"A fancy breakfast every morning. A massage in the couple's room in the spa."

"Oh, my goodness. I'm in heaven. Are we really going to be here for two full days?"

"Yes, we are." He'd chosen a hotel that was near the zoo since that was where Dana wanted to go on their honeymoon. "Champagne and chocolate-covered strawberries are also part of the package. But I told them to bring a bottle of sparkling cider, too."

She grinned. "For your preggers wife."

Damn, she was cute. At the wedding she'd drunk water during the toast. "I also told them to replace the strawberries with cherries."

"So that's the cherry treat you mentioned earlier." She waggled her eyebrows. "How decadent of you."

A knock sounded at the door, and Eric prepared to answer the summons. But before he walked away, he motioned for Dana to wait for him, on the bed, just as she was.

After everything arrived and there would be no more interruptions, Eric returned to Dana with the room service tray.

"Should we have this now or later?" he asked.

"Now." She sat forward. "Then we can mess around with the taste of extra goodness on our lips."

"I like how you think." He opened the cider and poured her a glass. He popped open the champagne for himself and sat next to her.

They sipped their drinks and ate the cherries, and every time he bit into one, he imagined burying himself deep inside her.

"These are delicious," she said, with a little orgasmic moan.

He ate another one, blood pumping its way to his groin. Being with her was going to be delicious. She was his cherry lover, his daisy bride, his go-for-it honeymoon partner. Maybe love wasn't part of the equation. But lust most certainly was.

This aspect of being married felt good, and he relished the allure that came with it. He leaned forward to kiss her. She met him halfway and their lips met. The taste of sensuality shivered through him.

The extra goodness.

He went to work on the pins in her hair, removing each little ornament with care. Her shiny blond locks, as soft and warm as sunlight, tumbled into his hands and slipped through his fingers.

"Let's stand up so I can undress you," he said. So he could peel away the silk to get to her skin.

She obliged him. She stood before him, looking like the bohemian bride he'd once called her. The dress had a zipper in back. He got behind her and worked it free. The gown opened with ease, exposing the curve of her spine and lacy white undergarments.

He came around to the front, anxious to take the dress completely off. As he slid the garment down, she smiled at him. He'd never met anyone who smiled as much as she did.

He kissed her, softly, just because it felt right. She kissed him, too, tugging him closer. By now, the dress was pooled at her feet.

They separated so she could step out and away from the fabric. But she didn't pick it up off the floor. She let Eric do that. He lifted it up and draped it across his hands. Then he walked to the closet and hung it up. He even rezipped it. He knew how hard she'd searched to find a gown that suited her, so he was doing what he could to treat it with reverence.

He returned to her, and she said, "You're so gallant."

"Not that gallant." He was too excited to give her undergarments the same special care.

Eric unhooked her bra and got rid of it. When he cupped her breasts, her nipples went instantly hard. He thumbed each one.

They kissed again. The hunger inside him turned to an ache. While their mouths were fused, he reached down and touched her in the most intimate of ways. He liked the feel of her flesh next to the lace panel of her panties. But when that sensation got to be too much, he removed her panties and discarded them.

She was naked. Lusciously bare. He resumed the foreplay, watching her as he did what he wanted to do. Her eyes were half-closed. She looked hot and dreamy.

Bridelike, he thought.

Did he look husbandlike, too, standing here in his tuxedo, giving her pleasure?

As he brought her to climax, she rewarded him with the same erotic little moan as when she'd been eating the chocolate cherries.

That was just about all he could take. In the thrill of the moment, he yanked off his own clothes, took her to bed and climbed on top of her. They kissed like mad, eager to consummate their vows.

They made love without protection. This time there was no need for a condom. They mated with flesh-to-flesh urgency.

He couldn't begin to count how many positions they tried or the things they did and redid to each other. All he knew was that their wedding night was on fire.

Dana lay there afterward, wondering what had hit her. A Mac Truck of a man, that's what—the hottest, sexiest, wildest man who ever existed.

She said, "I'm never going to be the same again."

He leaned on his elbow. "It was pretty crazy."

"It was positively sinful." She rolled onto her elbow, too, trying to steady herself. "We should do that again sometime."

"If we dare."

"I do kind of feel like I'm going to die."

Darkness flashed in his eyes. "Don't say that, Dana."

Her heart clenched. "Oh, I'm sorry. I didn't mean it literally. I was just, you know…"

"Yeah, I know. But it's tough to hear, even jokingly. I couldn't bear to lose another wife."

She blinked at him. She knew that he didn't want to be married and that he'd wed her out of duty, yet somewhere deep inside, he was already worried about losing her? It made her feel more attached to him. "You're not going to lose me."

He backpedaled. "I shouldn't have made a fuss. You can make whatever jokes you want. If you feel like you're going to die after great sex, then we should just laugh it off."

True. But neither of them was laughing. At this point, Dana wasn't sure how she was supposed to deal with his emotions. This was their first night as husband and wife, and already she was fretting about how to interact with him.

Fix the broken? Good luck with that, she told herself.

She changed the subject. "I'm excited about going to the zoo tomorrow."

"That's good. I want you to enjoy yourself."

"I love zoos. Won't it be fun when we can take Sweet Bean when he or she is older?"

"We used to take Kaley there when she was little."

We. Him and his other wife. Normally Dana didn't mind him making references to Corrine. But at the moment, she wished that she had Eric all to herself. Still, it was foolish to expect him to stop referring to his past, especially since he'd been doing it all along. Besides, wasn't it better for him to talk openly, rather than keep his memories bottled up inside?

"What were Kaley's favorite animals at the zoo?" she asked, encouraging him to say whatever he wanted.

He rewarded her with a smile. "The monkeys. She used to mimic them."

"I can see Kaley doing that. Even now."

He laughed a little. "She is expressive."

"What about Corrine? What animal did she favor?"

He seemed to be thinking back on it. "She liked the big cats."

"I can see why. You're rather big and catlike yourself."

"Are you flirting with me, Miss Cherry?"

She waved her new diamond, reminding him that she was a properly married woman now. "The name's *Mrs*. Cherry, and yes I am."

"That sounds weird, doesn't it? You being a Mrs." He went serious. "Mrs. Reeves." He tilted his head. "Are you going to use my last name or keep your own?"

"Truthfully, I hadn't really thought about it. Maybe I'll do it the hyphenated way. Dana Peterson-Reeves. That has a nice ring to it."

He didn't comment on whether he liked the sound of it. But he did reach out to skim his fingers down her arm.

"What's your favorite animal at the zoo?" he asked.

She appreciated the question. She appreciated the warmth of his touch, too. "The penguins. I like how they waddle."

"You'll be waddling before too long."

She poked him in the ribs. "Is the daddy-to-be teasing the woman he impregnated? Where are your manners?"

"It's fun teasing you."

"Then by all means, tease away." She liked this side of him. She liked it very much. Eric could be adorably playful when the mood struck him.

"I'll buy you a toy penguin tomorrow. I'm sure they'll have them in the gift shop."

"Thank you. That will make tomorrow even more special." Encouraged by his romantic behavior, she curled up next to him. Maybe fixing him wouldn't be that hard. Maybe he would settle into being her husband because he was naturally the husband type.

"Dana?"

"Yes?"

"I just wanted to tell you that I removed my wedding picture with Corrine from the mantel."

"You did?" She'd assumed that it was going to remain as it was. "Where did you put it?"

"In a box that has a bunch of other old photos. I knew it wasn't right to leave it up anymore. I even told Corrine it's what I should do, out of respect to you. I talked to her about it when I was at her gravesite."

"Thank you for thinking of me." As for him telling Corrine, she simply accepted that as part of the status quo.

"Ready to sleep now?" he asked.

She nodded, and he turned out the light.

While they settled into a spooning position, Dana closed her eyes, anxious to wake up with her husband by her side.

Eric got up before Dana and headed for the shower. Afterward, he prepared to order the fancy breakfast that came with the hotel package, but when he returned to bed and saw his wife, he stalled. She looked positively green.

She said, "I normally keep crackers by the bed, but I was having such a good time with you last night, I forgot to get them out of my luggage. And now I'm so nauseous I don't want to move."

"I'll get them." He tore into her suitcase and rummaged around. Her stuff was crammed in there. "I can't find them."

"Keep looking."

He finally located the saltines and brought them to her. He opened the box, too. He remembered how ill Corrine had gotten from the cancer treatments. But he warned himself not to panic. Dana's sickness was associated with life, not death.

But it still affected him, stirring up horrific memories. He wanted to make Dana feel better. He wanted to do something besides sit here and watch her take birdlike bites.

"How long does it take to go away?" he asked.

"Twelve weeks, they say. But I don't really know for sure."

"I meant each morning."

"It varies. Some women have bouts of it all day. I can't even imagine that."

He touched a hand to her brow. He felt helpless, and he despised that feeling. "Do you want anything else?"

"Sometimes hot tea helps."

"I'll make some." He hurried up with the task, fixing what he hoped was a mild brew.

He held out the cup and she took tiny sips.

"If I get up and run to the bathroom, you better move out of my way."

"I will. But if you want someone to hold your hair back while you throw up, I can do that, too."

She actually smiled. "That's the sweetest, ickiest thing a man has ever said to me."

"I just want you to be okay."

"Then tell Sweet Bean to knock it off."

"Knock it off," he said to her stomach.

She laughed, then moaned. "Oh, God. Laughing wasn't a good idea."

"I'm sorry."

"Just don't talk to me for a while."

He sat in a chair near the bed. By now she was bunched into a ball.

She gave up the fight and raced past him and into the bathroom. He would have preferred to hold her hair back than to sit here and do nothing. He could hear her retching.

He had to keep reminding himself that it was the baby and not anything serious. But his experience with Corrine wasn't helping the logical side of his brain to cope with having a sick wife.

Dana emerged a short while later, with her skin pale and her face damp from where she'd obviously splashed water on it.

She said, "I should be all right now."

She didn't look all right to him. "We're not going to the zoo today."

"Don't spoil my fun. I just need to rest for a bit." She got back into bed. "I was like this yesterday morning, and by late afternoon, I was walking down the aisle like a goddess. I swear, Eric, I'll be fine."

She spoke the truth. An hour later, she was hungry for breakfast. So he ordered it, and when it arrived, she ate like a little piggy. He'd never been so glad to see a woman wolf down her food.

"Told ya," she said. "I'm the picture of pregnant health."

And he was the picture of a guy too freaked out to be in this situation. His nerves were nearly shot. "I don't even want to consider what's going to happen later on."

"What do you mean?"

"When you're in labor and having those horrible contractions." He'd seen reenactments of childbirth on TV with wives yelling at their husbands and blaming them for the pain. "I don't think I'll be able to handle you screaming like a banshee."

"I'm too good-natured for that."

"You think you're going to be the exception?"

She flicked a chip of toast at him. "Yep."

He shook his head. She was something else. "I'm not having a food fight with you." He was too freaked out for that, too.

"Then for goodness' sakes, have a drink." She cracked open the mini bar and spiked his orange juice with a shot of vodka.

They both looked at the cocktail and laughed. It was absurd to be presented with a screwdriver at this time of the day. But even so, he went ahead and belted it back, using it as a reward for surviving his first morning of having a pregnant wife.

Dana and Eric walked around the zoo, and although she was enjoying their surroundings, she was still aware of how her pregnancy was affecting him. She didn't know what to do to get him to loosen up, at least not completely. With Eric, there was always an underlying edge.

"Are you ready for some ice cream?" he asked.

"I'm always ready for something sweet."

"I'll get it. You can sit here and relax." He motioned to a bench near the zebra habitat.

"You don't need to keep babying me."

"I'm not. I'm just offering to get the ice cream."

She decided not to argue the point. Sometimes it was easier to just go along with him and see where it led. "Make it a double scoop of chocolate."

"Will do."

He walked away, and she sat on the bench and gazed

at the zebras. She could see their black-and-white bodies through the greenery that filled their enclosure.

He returned with two sugar cones, piled with soft serve ice cream. His was vanilla.

They ate in silence, until he said, "I know an interesting fact about zebras."

"You do? What?"

"Not all of them live in harems or herds. There's a species where the males are solitary and the females come and go. When a foal is born into this type of society, the mother walks around her newborn so it will see only her stripe pattern. It's part of an imprinting process and is necessary for survival. The foal has to recognize its mother because no other female will adopt it."

"The imprinting is sweet, but the fact that they are unadoptable is sad. Thank goodness it isn't that way with humans."

"If it was, I wouldn't have Kaley, and I couldn't imagine life without her."

She couldn't imagine him without his daughter, either. "Zebras always reminded me of merry-go-rounds."

"When I was little, I used to associate them with striped gum."

She smiled. "Doesn't that come with temporary tattoos now?"

"I have no idea. I haven't chewed it since I was a kid. But man, I used to go to town on it then, one piece after another."

"Because it loses its flavor so fast."

"That's what was so cool about it. The quick, strong flavor burst."

"It's fun thinking of you as a kid. What other things were you into?"

"I'm a product of the seventies and the eighties, so I was into all sorts of goofy stuff, I guess. Mostly I was part of the skate and surf culture."

"There's nothing goofy about that. I can see you doing both."

"Sometimes I miss surfing."

"You should take it up again."

"I don't know. It's been a while. But I'll always have a fondness for the beach. That will never change."

She nodded. She knew how much he loved the sand and the surf. The pier, too. "You're a California boy."

"And now you're a California girl, too."

"By way of Ohio." She thought about his other wife. "Was Corrine born here?"

"Yes. She was from L.A., same as me."

"You two got married when you were twenty and adopted Kaley when you were twenty-four. When did you know for sure that Corrine couldn't conceive? How long did it take to find out?"

"We tried for about two years, then we decided to see a doctor about it and that's when they ran some tests and discovered that she was infertile. She was devastated at first, but then she figured that she was meant to be an adoptive mom, especially since she came from an adoptive family herself."

Dana glanced at the zebras. It didn't surprise her that Eric knew what he knew about them. That sort of information would've stuck in his mind, given his experience. "Why couldn't she conceive? What was wrong?"

"It was the result of an infection she had when she was younger. But she didn't realize how severe it was or that it caused infertility. She always had a lot of female problems. She was just used to that sort of thing."

He frowned at his ice cream. "I think that's why she didn't recognize the signs of her cancer."

Dana still didn't know what type it was. "You've never told me about it before."

"It was uterine cancer. She'd already gone through an early menopause, and she thought the symptoms were related to that. She didn't see a doctor right away like she should have. But she was still determined to beat it. She fought a good fight. But it was awful, seeing her so sick."

"Is that why my morning sickness bothers you so much?"

He nodded. "I know it's not the same, but it still gives me the same feeling."

"It's definitely not the same. In a few weeks, I'm going to be right as rain. Waddling like a penguin later on, but that's how it's supposed to be."

He laughed a little. "The voice of motherhood."

"Darn straight." She was glad their conversation had turned light. She was also glad that they were tackling the morning sickness issue. "So no more worrying about me."

"I'll decide when it's time to stop worrying."

She waved her ice cream around. "Can you be any more stubborn?"

"And can you be any messier? You have chocolate on your nose, Dana."

"I do not."

"You do, too."

She took her napkin and dabbed at her nose. Sure enough, she came away with chocolate. She burst into a giggle. "You could have told me earlier."

"It just happened." He held his cone out to her. "Want to put some vanilla on it, too?"

"Maybe just a little." She took a bite instead.

"Hey!" He pulled it away from her, and they laughed like a couple of kids.

But shouldn't they be acting like kids? They were at the zoo, after all. "We still have a lot more animals to see."

"And a toy penguin to buy," he reminded her.

She grinned and gave him a chocolate-flavored kiss, and he kissed her back, making it ridiculously noisy. In spite of how the day had begun, it was turning into a fun-filled adventure and just what she'd hoped for.

The entire honeymoon was special. Dana enjoyed every moment of it. But it was over now, and she was back at her house, preparing to move in with Eric. Most of her belongings were already packed, but she still had last-minute things to throw into boxes.

Eric was at work, but Candy was there, keeping her company until the movers arrived. Since there was no room for Dana's furniture at Eric's house, it would be going into storage until she could sell it.

"I'm going to miss my stuff," she said. Her colorful dining table and mismatched chairs, her quaint little loveseat, the coat rack that held her shawls, the shabby chic dresser in her bedroom. "Eric's stuff is nice, but it isn't me."

"So toss some of your style into it. Scatter your knickknacks around."

"I can't do that without consulting him first. Can you imagine if he came home and saw that I'd made changes to his house?"

"Eric is the one who suggested that you study interior design. Surely, he's expecting you to redecorate a bit."

"He's expecting me to make a mess. That much I know. He thinks that I'll leave my clothes all over the bedroom."

Candy smirked. "Because you will."

"Thanks for the vote of confidence."

"I meant that in the kindest of ways."

Distracted, Dana picked up the stuffed penguin he'd bought her. "I keep thinking about how I need to fix him."

"I knew you would be."

"Sometimes he's so amazing and romantic. And other times, he's so troubled and distant." She cuddled the penguin. "I've actually been having fantasies about what falling in love with him would be like. Does that surprise you?"

"Truthfully? It doesn't." Candy's sigh sounded like a cross between pity and wonder. "What woman wouldn't want to fall for her big handsome tortured husband? The same guy who surprised her with an antique ring on her wedding day and arranged a spellbinding honeymoon."

"When you put it that way…" Dana laughed.

Candy laughed, too, even if they both seemed to know that it wasn't funny. Dana and Eric hadn't entered into a union based on love.

Uncomfortable with the thought, she said, "Do you think it's weird that he visits Corrine's grave as often as he does?"

"Not if it gives him peace."

"Maybe I should go and confide in her, too."

"Confide in her about what? Fantasizing about falling in love with her husband? He's your husband, too."

"I just think I'd feel better about it if she knew."

"Do you think she's really going to be able to hear you?"

"I don't know." She quit cuddling the penguin, setting it off to the side. "Do you think I'm going to be able to handle falling in love with him if it happens?"

"You can handle anything, Dana."

"Even being in love with a man who doesn't love me?" The question packed a punch. It was the very thing Candy had experienced in her own get-pregnant-get-hitched marriage. Only sadly for her, the baby was gone and so was the husband she'd loved. "You know better than anyone what that's like."

"Which is why I'm not a fair judge. But you're stronger than I am, so I'm going to vote yes. Plus you're so charming and cool, if you love him, he won't have a choice but to cave in and love you, too."

Dana reached out to hug her friend. She couldn't have said anything nicer. "I'm going to miss you way more than I'm going to miss my furniture."

"You're not putting me in storage, silly. But I'm going to miss seeing you every day, too."

"Rent this place to someone great, okay?"

"No one is going to be as great as you are."

They hugged again, and the movers arrived. After the truck was packed, Dana said goodbye to Candy and met up with the movers at the storage facility. Soon after that, she went to Eric's house, where they unloaded the rest of her things.

Once she was alone, she wandered in and out of each room. Already she was getting cabin fever. Or suburbia fever, as it were, with the sudden urge to flee.

But Candy was right. This was her residence now,

too, and she needed to relax and make her presence known, for more than the messes everyone was in agreement that she was going to make.

So she called Eric when she knew he would be on a break, asking him if it was okay for her to make a few changes around the house.

He gave her his blessing, so she started the process of digging through her boxes, eager to spice things up.

Chapter Ten

Eric opened the front door and entered a much more colorful house, which was what he'd expected.

The back of the sofa was draped with a printed throw and a shimmery vase sat on the end table. Everywhere he looked some sort of gypsy doodad had been added: candles, incense burners, glass statuary.

But the part he hadn't expected was the artwork prominently displayed above the fireplace. The pieces belonged to him, not to Dana. He'd kept them stored in the garage, where she'd obviously found them.

He struggled to grasp how it made him feel, other than newly married and confused.

Not only had she made changes to the interior of the place, she was making dinner. He smelled something delicious in the air. He welcomed the meal. The artwork, not so much.

Just then, a ponytailed Dana appeared from the kitchen to greet him. She bounced into the living room, wearing a fifties-style apron over her jeans and T-shirt. He imagined her saying, "Hi, honey, how was your day?"

But instead, she searched his expression and asked, "So, what do you think?"

He assumed she was talking about the house. But because he wasn't ready to comment on the artwork, he focused on her attire. "That's a cute look on you. Is it from a thrift store? Did you get it recently?"

"What? Oh, this?" She smoothed the apron. "I bought it ages ago. Come on, Eric, what do you think of the way I redecorated? If you hate it, I'll put it back the way it was. But I'm hoping that you'll appreciate it."

"I like the gypsy stuff. You made it work in here. But what in the world possessed you to put those paintings up?"

"Because Kaley texted me earlier and when I told her I was doing a bit of redecorating, she said that I should check out the artwork in the garage. That there were some pieces that I would probably love. And I do love them. They're phenomenal."

"Did she also tell you that they're old paintings of mine?"

"They're your work? No, she didn't mention that. But that's even better. Oh, Eric. They're amazing."

He winced. "They're just average landscapes."

"Average? Are you kidding? They're misty and moonlit. As soon as I saw them, I felt as if I was being transported to an enchanted realm where powerful lords and delicate ladies were going to sweep me into their beautiful shadows."

He furrowed his brow, pleased by her praise, but uncomfortable about it, too. "You sound like Corrine. She used to say they that made her feel magical. She never understood why I didn't think they were worthy of being displayed."

"Really? She said almost the same thing as I did?"

"Yes, she did."

"Then there you go. Two women can't be wrong."

"Three women. Kaley always wanted me to put them up, too."

"Ah, then that explains why she told me about them. She loves the changes I made, by the way. I sent her some pictures."

He wasn't surprised. His daughter wasn't a creature of habit. She thrived on change. "I'm glad she's happy about it." This would always be Kaley's home, too, the place where she grew up.

"What do you think of the seashells?"

"What?"

"Below the paintings." She gestured to the mantel. "I put them there because you love the beach."

He saw what she meant. She'd placed a grouping of shells where his old wedding picture had been. She'd filled the space with something reminiscent of his past, yet connected to his future since his first date with Dana had taken place at the beach.

"That's clever," he told her. She had a way of making everything fit somehow. "You're going to make a great decorator."

"Thanks." She beamed. "I put a romantic memento from our wedding in the bedroom."

He doubted that it was a photograph because they hadn't gotten the professional ones back yet and the images their friends and family had taken weren't the best quality. Plus why would she have called it a memento and not just said that it was a picture?

"Do you want to see what it is?" she asked.

"Yes, of course." She'd piqued his curiosity.

The bedroom, he discovered, was a disaster. She had open boxes everywhere with the contents spilling out of them.

"I haven't finished unpacking," she said.

So he gathered. If there was a wedding memento in here, he sure as heck didn't see it. But he could see how she'd crammed her clothes into the closet, the hangers poking out at warped angles and the weight of the rod sagging from the extra weight.

She followed his line of sight. "Those aren't even all of my clothes. I don't know where I'm going to put the rest of them."

"We can get a portable closet or a big armoire or something. So, where's this romantic thing?"

"On the dresser."

He glanced in the direction she'd mentioned. It was the bride and groom topper from their cake, with her daisy hairpins clipped together in a circle around it.

Eric's pulse dipped and dived. She'd created a sweet and sexy reminder of that day. And night. He would never forget removing those pins from her hair.

"That's a nice memento," he said.

"I thought so, too."

She moved closer. They probably should have kissed, but they didn't. Suddenly, everything seemed awkward. They'd only been married for a few days and now that the honeymoon was over and they were locked in a quiet moment, they didn't know how to behave around each other.

She broke the tension. "I've got chicken and potatoes in the oven. That's what we'll be having for dinner."

"Sounds good. Smells great, too."

"It should ready in about twenty minutes."

"I'll meet you in the kitchen. I'm going to change."

"Okay." She left him alone.

He maneuvered around the boxes and made his way to the dresser. After he retrieved some comfortable clothes, he closed the drawers, and the vibration rattled the cake topper. The bride and groom wobbled and fell over. Was that a sign of things to come? A message that they were fooling themselves by being married? He didn't know what to think, other than it was all too new to tell.

Eric righted the figures and changed into a T-shirt and drawstring sweatpants. Rather than meet her in the kitchen sooner than necessary, he attempted to organize the boxes, moving them out of the walkway, along with their spilled contents.

Finally he entered the kitchen. Dana was bustling around in her old-fashioned apron, preparing a salad to go along with the main course.

She did a zillion things at once, he realized. Within the course of a day that wasn't even over yet, she'd moved into his place, half unpacked, rearranged the house and fixed a hearty meal.

He walked over to the window where she'd placed a sun catcher. He gazed outside. In the backyard, wind chimes were hanging from the roof of the patio cover, and the only way for her to have accomplished that would have been to use a ladder.

"I can't believe you took a chance like that," he said.
She turned toward him. "What?"

"Climbed up there."

"Pregnant women aren't invalids."

"You could have fallen."

"You're being a worrywart."

He ignored her comment. "I think you need to start taking it easy. Between work and school and your efforts here at the house, you'll run yourself ragged."

"I like keeping busy, and I'll pace myself when I need to."

"Maybe you should quit your job." At least that would eliminate the hours she spent on her feet at the diner.

"Seriously? You're going overboard."

"I just want you to take care of yourself."

"I promise I will, okay? I'll take a long maternity leave when the time gets closer."

"You're not even out of your first trimester yet. That's going to take forever."

"The baby will be here soon enough." She removed the chicken from the oven. "In fact, it wouldn't hurt to bandy about some names."

"Other than Sweet Bean?"

"Yup."

He helped her set the table, and she put the food down.

"What do you think?" she asked, as they sat across from each other.

"Everything looks delicious." She'd even made a refreshing gelatin dessert that he was eager to try.

"Thanks, but I was talking about the names."

His thoughts drifted to a custom from his culture.

"In the old Cherokee way, a boy is referred to as a bow and a girl is a sifter."

"Like a bow from a bow and arrow and a sifter that sifts flour?"

He nodded. "Males are associated with being hunters and providers and females are associated with nourishing the family and giving life. There's even a Cherokee incantation for childbirth that relates to the bow and sifter tradition."

"What is the incantation supposed to do?"

"Make the birth easier."

She smiled. "Then maybe you should start saying it instead of worrying about me."

"It's not something the father does. It's part of a ritual done by the medicine person or midwife delivering the baby. I don't know the exact words, but it encourages the little boy or girl, the bow or sifter, to hurry and come out."

"A quick birth would be nice."

"A quicker pregnancy would be nice, too."

She smiled again. "It takes as long as it takes, Eric. You need to be more patient."

"I'm trying. I swear I am." But he feared the months ahead of them were going to seem like a lifetime.

She cut into her chicken. "I asked you this before, but I'm just wondering how you feel now. Do you want to know ahead of time if we're having a boy or girl? Do you want to find out on my next ultrasound? Or wait until it's born?"

"I think I'd like to know ahead of time. Then we can start a list of names, and you can decorate the nursery accordingly, too."

"I was planning on doing zoo animals for the nursery, if that's okay with you. I figured it would work either way, for a boy or a girl."

"Then we'll go with zoo animals and see what shows up on the ultrasound later."

"Or doesn't show up. If it's a girl, you don't see anything. But sometimes they can't tell at all, if the baby is in a position where those parts are hidden."

"I hope we can tell."

"Me, too." She tasted her food. "Maybe we should explain bows and sifters to the ultrasound technician. So instead of saying it's a boy or a girl, they can say it's a bow or a sifter to the expectant parents."

"That would be funny, wouldn't it?"

She nodded, and they both smiled. Then she asked, "Are you going to help with the nursery?"

"Do you want me to help?"

"Of course. I totally want you to be involved."

He thought about how he could make himself useful, other than putting the crib together. "I can paint pictures of the animals directly on the wall."

She leaned forward in her seat. "That's a great idea. Way better than using stencils or borders."

"The Cherokee symbolism of each animal could be used, too. For example, I can paint 'introspection' next to the bear, and 'dreaming' beside the lizard. We can pick and choose what animals to use based on their spiritual totems."

"I love that." Apparently she loved it so much, she nearly knocked over her water. But she caught the glass before it spilled.

"Good save, Dana."

"Thanks." She sat back and readjusted her napkin

on her lap. "How involved with Kaley were you when she was a baby?"

"What do you mean?"

"Did you get up and feed her in the middle of the night? Did you change diapers? Or did Corrine do most of those things?"

"We shared responsibility." He wrinkled his nose. "Although I would have been more than happy to pass the dirty-diaper buck."

She laughed. "Seriously? Who wouldn't? But if you did it for Kaley, then you're going to do it for Sweet Bean, too."

"Yes, but just remember how much younger I was back then."

"What's that supposed to mean? That your gag reflexes have gotten more pronounced?" She rolled her eyes at his lame excuse. "You're not too old to wipe a baby's bottom, Eric."

"Listen to you, the authority. How many diapers have you changed?"

"Well, none actually. But—"

"None? As in zip? Zero? Nada?" He wasn't going to let her talk her way out of this one. "Didn't you ever babysit or anything?"

"I babysat plenty. Just not kids who weren't potty trained."

"Oh, this is rich. I'll be teaching you how to do everything."

"Really, smarty? You're going to teach me to breast-feed? That I'd like to see."

"At least I know how to bottle feed."

"That's not the same thing."

"It will be if you use a pump or whatever it is that

breast-feeding mothers do. Then I'll be bottle feeding like I used to, and teaching you how to do it, too."

She kept the silly banter going. "I'll already know how to do it by then."

"Because I would have showed you." He mock pounded his chest. "The gorilla king of dads."

She made a goofy face. "Nice try, but times have changed, pop. You're probably going to have to learn some of this stuff over again."

No doubt, which he thought was downright scary. He liked the idea of her breast-feeding, though. He thought it sounded warm and gentle.

Dana asked, "When Kaley was offered to you, did you know that she was going to be a girl?"

"Not at first. But later we did."

"What made you decide on her name?"

"I wanted to name the baby after my mom, with something that was similar but not the same. My mother's name was Kaleen. So Corrine suggested Kaley."

After a pause, Dana asked, "Where is she buried, Eric?"

The question threw him off track. They'd gone from names to burial plots? "Mom was cremated and scattered in the mountains. Dad was, too. It was what they wanted."

"I was talking about Corrine."

"Why do you want to know where she is?"

"Because I want to visit her sometime."

"You don't need to do that."

"I'm not asking to go with you. I would never intrude on your solitude like that. I just want to go on my own."

"What for?"

"To bring her flowers from my new garden."

"What new garden?"

"The one I'm going to plant in the backyard, with your approval, of course. You wouldn't mind if I created a garden, would you?"

"You can plant as many flowers as you want. But I'd rather not have you go to Corrine's grave." He wasn't ready to share that part of his life with her. It didn't matter that Dana was talking about going by herself. To him, it still seemed like an invasion of his privacy. "I'd prefer to keep things as they are."

She seemed disappointed, but she didn't push it beyond his limits. She merely said, "Maybe you'll feel differently later. Maybe you'll change your mind."

"Maybe." But for now, he just couldn't agree to it.

After they finished the food on their plates, she asked, "Are you ready for dessert?"

"Yes, please." He appreciated that she'd made a nice treat to go along with their meal, but mostly he was relieved that she'd changed the subject.

"Do you want whipped cream on yours?"

"That sounds good."

She studied him for a moment. Then she said, "I need to get it." She went into the kitchen and returned with the canned kind. "This is my favorite. It's always so fun to use. See. Now watch." She served him a generous helping of the colorful gelatin mold and decorated it with a smiley face made of the frothy topping.

He looked at her artwork and laughed. She decorated hers with the same design, except with dotted eyelashes and fuller lips, implying that hers was a girl.

Eric laughed again. "You certainly know your way around that stuff."

"You have no idea." She shot some straight into her mouth.

He shook his head. Dana was always doing something wonderfully weird. "I used to do that when I was a kid. But I used to get in trouble for it. That and drinking milk from the carton. That used to drive my mom nuts."

"My mom used to correct me all the time, too. But it didn't help." She grinned and offered him the can. "Want to misbehave now? No one will scold you for it."

"No, thanks. I'll stick to what's in my bowl." He delved into the dessert and ate several spoonfuls, smearing the face.

"I put that on there because I wanted to make you laugh. You were frowning before I went into the kitchen to get the whipped cream and you were still scowling when I came back."

He cocked his head. "I was?"

She nodded. "You frown when you're not even aware of it."

If he'd been frowning, it was a subconscious reaction leftover from their graveyard discussion. "I didn't mean to seem as if I was mad."

"I didn't think you were mad. You're just guarded."

Guarded was an accurate word to describe him. That was definitely how he felt. "I'm sorry, Dana."

"No need to apologize. But I think we need to redo that." She refreshed his dessert with another happy face, replacing the one he'd smeared.

He shooed her hand away, but he did it playfully. He couldn't help but be amused. "If you keep doing that every time I take a bite, I'll make a pig of myself and end up with a stomachache."

"Then you better smile more, Eric."

"And you better quit being such a pest." For good measure, he zeroed in on a kiss, cupping the back of her head and capturing her lips. She moaned and returned his affection eagerly.

So eagerly, she climbed onto his lap, and he forgot about gelatin molds or whipped cream happy faces or anything except the sweetly intoxicating taste of his wife.

Three weeks later, Eric awakened on a Saturday morning, without Dana by his side. She was probably in the bathroom, retching her brains out. The twelve-week mark had passed, but her morning sickness hadn't improved. Eric frowned. Maybe her doctor could give her something for it. Maybe next time he should go with her to the appointment.

In some ways he was becoming accustomed to having her as his wife, and in other ways he remained unsettled. His emotions were all over the board. Dana moved at such a different pace than he did. When she wasn't sick, she was bursting with energy, spinning around him like a sparkly little dust devil. Sometimes she just plain wore him out. Yet being around her was exciting, too.

In search of Dana, he got out of bed and checked the bathroom. Upon finding it empty, he went into the kitchen to see if she was there. Nope. Kitchen was empty, too.

Eric started a pot of coffee, wondering where she was. She was never up and about at this time of day, not with how nauseous she always was.

While he waited for the coffee to brew, he poured a glass of orange juice. He also opened the curtain on the kitchen window, then spotted Dana in the backyard, digging in the dirt. Was she planting her flower garden? Now? First thing in the morning?

He went to the sliding glass door, pulled back the blinds and headed outside. As he got closer, he noticed that both cats were hanging out with her. The tabbies picked through the soil she'd unearthed, making muddy paw prints in the areas she'd dampened with the hose.

When Eric walked over to her, she glanced up and cupped a gloved hand over her brow, creating a sunshield.

"Guess what?" she said. "This is the first morning I woke up without feeling sick."

"So you went to the nursery and bought a bunch of plants?"

"I figured it was time to create the garden." She smiled, her eyes as blue as the sky. "My way of celebrating." She stood up and dusted off her jeans. "Your juice looks good." She removed her gloves and stuffed them in her back pocket. "May I have a sip?"

He held out the glass. He hadn't even realized that he'd brought it outside with him.

She drank some and passed it back. "Aren't you happy for me? No more nausea."

He was extremely happy that she was well. But the garden looked like a major undertaking. "I still wish you would take it easy, Dana."

"Are you kidding? I feel like a million bucks." She made a quick spin to showcase her health. With a deliberate grin, she pointed out what she planned to do. "I'm going to fill this planter with perennials. And over there, I'm going to dig up the grass and replace it with a row of mazelike hedges. And that spot in the corner is reserved for a cozy bench and a quaint little walkway, with stepping stones and fluffy foliage." She turned toward the patio. "I was thinking of adding more potted plants, too."

"I can't let you do all of that by yourself." She wasn't planting a garden. She was landscaping the whole dang yard. "I'll do the heavy labor."

She clapped her hands together. "You're going to help me? Oh, that's wonderful. With the two of us, we could complete it this weekend."

"The entire project?"

She nodded, bright-eyed and bushy-tailed. "Maybe we could get a mini fountain, too. A smaller version of Tinkle. I really miss him."

And he missed the order that used to be his life. But he didn't miss the loneliness. With Dana, he was never lonely. She was a constant companion, always delving into some sort of mind-spinning mischief.

He said, "We're not going to be able to get all of it done this weekend."

"How long do you think it will take?"

"Between an old guy like me and a pregnant lady like you, two, maybe three weekends."

She laughed at his description of them. "The important part is enjoying ourselves." She snagged his juice and drank the last of it. "Come on, old guy, let's get started on that fun."

"I'm still in my pajamas."

She gave him the once over. "Sweatpants and a wrinkled T-shirt? That's perfect garden attire. All you need is a pair of work gloves."

"I've got some in the garage."

"Then go get them. Time's a wasting."

"I think I liked you better when you were throwing up every morning."

She laughed again. Beautiful chaos. "Snap to, Eric."

He shifted his stance. Moving quickly was going to require coffee, but thankfully it was already made. Still, there was the matter of food. "What about breakfast? I need to eat."

"So go grab something and hurry back."

He grumbled on his way to the fridge. She was henpecking him already. But as he slapped a sandwich together, he smiled.

He was looking forward to pleasing her and making the yard as wonderful as he could.

The project took two and a half weekends, and when it was complete, they stood in amazement and admired it.

"It's everything I imagined," she said.

Eric agreed. It was definitely her vision: the profusion of color, the soft, inviting warmth, the water trickling from the fountain, the little cove and walkway.

She took his hand and led him to the bench, where they sat and gazed at it from another angle.

"I could sit here forever," she said.

"I really like this spot, too."

She leaned forward and kissed him. Her mouth tasted like caramel and peppermint. She'd been eating candy for most of the day. He deepened the kiss and put his hand on her tummy. She was nearly four months along now, and she had a tiny pooch. Not enough to look pregnant, but Eric knew what her body had been like before Sweet Bean had made the scene.

After the kiss ended, she rested her head on his shoulder.

"Are you tired?" he asked.

"A little. But I'm content, too."

So was he. He gazed at the plants and frowned. Not so content that he'd stopped going to Corrine's grave. And not so content that he was willing to share her resting place with Dana. Luckily, she hadn't brought it up again. But he suspected that it was still on her mind, especially since her intent had been to bring Corrine flowers from this very garden.

"You're going to be off for summer break soon," she said.

"One of the perks of being a teacher. And Ryan and Victoria's wedding is coming up." He thought about the event they would be attending. "You're going to love their farmhouse. Ryan's veterinary practice is on the property, and he has chickens, a horse and a miniature cow."

"I'm anxious to see it."

"We'll be staying there during the wedding, so you'll have plenty of time to get acquainted with it. In fact, they asked if you and Kaley and I would stay a bit longer and housesit for them while they're on their honeymoon."

"Really? So we'll get to feed the chickens and the cow and the horse?"

He nodded. "They also have two dogs. But Kaley will probably be in charge of them. They follow her around like lovesick puppies."

"That's sweet. You know, I've been thinking that I'm going to cut back a bit at the diner. The manager already hired a new girl to fill in for me, so I might as well take advantage of it."

"Good. I'm glad. You know how I feel about you pushing yourself too hard."

"Yes, I'm well aware of how protective you are. You barely let me do anything on the yard."

"I let you do plenty."

"Not as much as I'm capable of doing." She was still resting her head against his shoulder. "It drives me crazy. But it's nice, too."

He fanned his fingers over her stomach. As a husband and father, it was his job to keep Dana and their child safe. To him, it was the most important role in a man's life, and Eric was taking it seriously.

Chapter Eleven

Summer arrived with a bit of June gloom, but the weather warmed up soon enough. And by now, Dana was definitely showing. Every time she looked in the mirror, she marveled at her cute little baby bump.

Eric entered the bedroom and stood behind her. She gazed at his reflection. They were leaving for Oregon today. They'd decided to drive instead of fly. Kaley would be riding along with them.

"I just know that you and Kaley are going to over pack," he said.

"Us girls gotta have our clothes."

"Tell me about it. If you get any more maternity dresses, we're going to have to move to a bigger house to make room for them."

"I can't help that my old clothes don't fit me anymore. And at least I buy cheap."

"The thrift store queen."

She struck a regal pose. "I like old things."

"Then it's a good thing you married me."

She reached back and nudged him. He was always making old-guy jokes. "Knock it off."

"I'm only going to get older, Dana."

"I'm going to get older, too."

"Yes, but you'll still always be sixteen years behind me."

"You know that doesn't matter to me." She would always adore her husband, at any age.

Adore him? Or love him? she asked herself.

At the moment, she didn't want to answer that question. She was anxious about seeing Ryan and Victoria and being immersed in how brightly their love shined.

She gazed at their reflections again.

"What's wrong?" he asked.

"Nothing," she lied. "We just have a lot going on." At least that wasn't a lie. After they returned from Oregon, she would be having the ultrasound that would most likely reveal Sweet Bean's gender. Plus, they were still in the middle of decorating the nursery. On top of that, Kaley and Candy had been talking about cohosting a baby shower for her and having it here at the house.

He said, "Don't let me forget to pack the garment bag that has my tux in it. Ryan would scalp me if I left it behind."

"You won't forget, but I'll remind you when we're loading up the car." Although this tuxedo was a different style than the one he'd worn to their wedding, he'd rented it at the same shop. "And Ryan would never scalp you."

"True." He put his arms around her, resting his hands

on the baby bump. "I'm the guy who raised his daughter."

She leaned back against him. Because he was making her want to melt, she locked her knees to keep from going dreamy.

She said, "Ryan told me that he didn't like you at first. That he was jealous because he thought you would end up with Victoria."

"Yeah, but he was way off the mark. Victoria and I were never attracted to each other."

"Did you know that she was in love with him when she was younger? Did she confide in you about it?"

"When I first met her? No. She kept those feelings a secret, even from him."

Dana drew a breath. A woman who'd been secretly in love wasn't the best topic for her to be discussing. But she'd started this conversation, so she was going to finish it.

She said, "At least Ryan made up for the past."

"He struggled with what he'd done for most of his life. He even married someone else. But he didn't love that woman enough to make it work, so she divorced him."

Dana didn't want to think about failed marriages, not while she was fighting her feelings for Eric. But she inquired about Ryan's ex, anyway. "What happened to her?"

"She got remarried a while ago. So, basically, it was a win-win for everyone. But they're all lucky it turned out that way. Not everyone is that lucky."

Was it luck or was it fate? Although Dana knew the difference, sometimes it seemed like the same thing. Besides, she was confused today.

"I'm going to go check the oil in the car," he said.

"Okay. I'll finish getting ready."

He nuzzled her shoulder, then walked away, leaving her feeling much too alone.

On the day they arrived at the farmhouse, Victoria and Ryan greeted them on the front porch.

Victoria took one look at Dana's protruding belly and said, "Oh, my goodness, check you out."

Dana smiled. "Sweet Bean is getting bigger."

Victoria leaned in to hug her. "After I gave Kaley up, I used to get sad whenever I saw a pregnant woman. But now it makes me joyous, and it's especially joyous to see you carrying Eric's child."

"Thank you. That means the world to me."

Their gazes met and held, and Dana wondered if Victoria was analyzing her, if she suspected that Dana might be in love with Eric.

No, that was foolish. How could Victoria suspect anything? She and Dana barely knew each other. But more importantly, Dana refused to obsess about her feelings.

But as the Oregon trip unfolded, she couldn't seem to help it. Ryan and Victoria's wedding was filled with love, just as Dana knew it would be.

The ceremony was in the evening, with twinkling lights and hundreds of candles that created a breathtaking ambience. The bride wore a stunning custom-made gown with Native American embellishments, in honor of the groom's tribe. He wore a tux, but he also had an Indian blanket draped around his shoulders. As part of their joining, they fed each other bits of foods from a traditional Paiute wedding basket.

While they recited their vows, their gazes were locked in sheer joy. There were no stumbling blocks, nothing keeping them from spending the rest of their lives together. The heartache from the past was over. Their grown daughter was sharing this moment with them. Kaley had never looked more beautiful. She wore a buckskin dress and carried a feather fan.

And Eric. The best man. Dana's heart filled with pride when she saw him standing at the gazebo altar, watching his daughter's birth parents become one. The blanket was now draped over both of their shoulders, sealing their union.

At the reception, a three-course dinner was served beneath a big white canopy. Throughout the meal, many of the guests tapped their drinking glasses with their silverware, prompting the bride and groom to kiss. Even Eric tapped his, joining in on the ritual. He presented a beautiful toast, too, reciting a Native blessing.

Later, when the newly married couple danced, all eyes were upon them. Eric Clapton's "Change the World" came on first. The DJ announced that Ryan and Victoria chose it because it was a special part of their long-ago and recent history.

As Dana watched them, she thought about her history with Eric. They didn't have a long-ago past. Everything was current. No, that wasn't true, she amended. She'd known him for a year before they slept together. He'd been her customer all that time, with an attraction brewing between them even then.

Once the other guests were invited to dance, Eric led her to the dance floor. Dana relished the feeling of being in his arms, and when he smiled at her, she admitted to herself, right then and there, that she was in love with her husband.

She lifted a hand to his cheek. Would he love her someday, too? Or would his heart be impossible to catch?

"Are you all right?" A stab of worry flashed in his eyes.

"I'm fine."

"Your hand feels clammy."

The hand on his cheek? "It does?"

"Yes." He covered it with his, as if he were trying to warm her up. "Should we sit down?"

"No. I want to keep dancing." To stay in his arms. "It feels good being here with you like this."

"Are you sure?" He didn't seem convinced. "Your hand is still so cold."

"Then hold me closer."

Eric did what she asked. He held her so incredibly close that she was able to mold her body against his. Dana wanted to tell him how she felt. She wanted to reveal that she loved him, but she couldn't bring herself to do it.

She was afraid of what his reaction would be, and she was rarely fearful of anything. Her motto had always been to attack life head on, but she couldn't seem to attack this situation.

"Will you make love with me tonight?" she asked.

"Of course I will. I always want to be intimate with you."

Sex, she thought. Passion. It was the emotional outlet that worked between them. Only from now on it was going to take on a different kind of emotion for her.

"I always want to be intimate with you, too," she

said. "And I'm feeling particularly amorous tonight." It was as close as she could come to saying that she loved him, without actually saying it.

"It's probably the wedding. The romantic vibe."

It was so much more than that, but she let him believe that the setting was instrumental in her behavior. "As soon as we go to our room, I want you to kiss me as hard as you can."

"I can kiss you right now." He lowered his head and put his lips softly against hers.

She moaned her frustration. "That was too light." She needed to numb her mind with more.

"I want to be light and gentle."

"Why can't you be hard and rough instead?"

He slipped his hand down to cradle her bump. "Because I want to be gentle with the mother of my child."

Her knees went weak. How could she argue with what he said? He was creating an illusion of love, drawing her into a need she couldn't deny.

Now she wanted it the way he wanted it, craving exactly what he was offering. She wanted to bask in each and every gentle touch, for as long as she could.

Later that night, Dana slid into bed with her husband. Being naked with him felt like silk over satin, like cream over the sweetest most succulent dessert.

She made soft girlish sounds, sighing while he kissed her.

He caressed her bare flesh, running his hands along her curves. Her figure was much fuller now, not only her stomach, but her hips, thighs and breasts, too.

He lowered his head to tongue one of her nipples,

and she ran her fingers through his hair, toying with the thickness.

"They're darker now," he said.

It took a second for his words to register. He was talking about her areolas and nipples.

"They're bigger, too," he said, dragging his tongue across the other one. "I like how they look. It's sexy."

"Then I hope they stay this way." She wanted to be sexy for the man she'd married. The man she loved.

Would this be the right time to tell him?

She squeezed her eyes shut. No. She couldn't do it. She couldn't tamper with the warmth of this moment. Eric was being the perfect lover, the perfect fantasy husband. If she told him and he drew away from her, she would lose this night forever.

She was going to wait until she was stronger, more emotionally equipped to say it. She would know, wouldn't she, when the time was right?

Heavens, she hoped so. It was all so new, so different, so unlike anything she'd ever experienced.

Clearly, this was the way Eric had felt about Corrine. The feeling he mourned. The woman he couldn't seem to forget.

Dana kept her eyes tightly closed. How could she compete with that? How could she cope with being in Corrine's shadow now that she'd fallen in love with Eric?

"Open your eyes," he said, as he pressed his fingers between her legs. "Look at me."

Look at him? Now? While he pleasured her? It should have been easy to comply with the request. But her eyelids felt weighted down, as if she couldn't handle the task.

He persisted. "I want us to connect when I make it happen for you."

"We are connecting."

"It's always better when we're looking at each other."

She forced herself to meet his gaze. He reacted by heightening her pleasure, by making her body scream for more.

"You're too good at this," she said.

"There's no such thing as being too good at something."

She arched beneath his touch. "It feels too good."

He kissed her while he made her shake and shiver, while she clung to him like a desperate reed in the wind.

But it didn't end there. After she went lax and her heart turned to jelly, he positioned her on her side and got behind her.

He entered her, deep and slow, pulling her into a prism of life-altering passion. He kissed her neck, her shoulders. He moved with masculine confidence, stroking her to another peak.

The room was spinning. Her world was changing. And there was nothing she could do about it.

Except embrace the wonder of Eric.

During the house-sitting phase of their trip, Eric and Kaley taught Dana how to care for the farm animals that lived on the property. Not only did she learn how to feed them, she also became proficient at gathering eggs, milking the cow and pasteurizing the milk. She thought it was fun, especially with her husband and his daughter as her trainers.

Today they were taking a break and spending a few hours in the woods that flanked the farmhouse. Only

Kaley wasn't with them. She was visiting with June, her Oregon friend, who was home from college for the summer.

"I really like it here," Dana said.

"So do I," Eric replied. "But I've always appreciated nature. I used to surf when I was younger, as you know, but I also hiked and camped. I still try to commune with Mother Earth however I can, even if it's in simple ways."

She thought he looked magnificent in this environment, with the trees towering above him like timber gods.

As his hair blew across his forehead, she itched to touch it. To distract herself, she glanced at the blanket they were sitting on. It was just a plain-colored throw, nothing like the one that had been used in the wedding earlier this week.

"I loved the Native influence in Ryan and Victoria's ceremony," she said. "I loved the way you toasted them with a Native blessing, too."

"Thank you. Ryan has been learning to bond with his culture. His Paiute mother died when he was just a boy, and he was raised by his Anglo father."

"He told me that his father passed away a few years ago and how they had a strained relationship."

"I've never had any of those issues in my family."

"Which parent of yours was Native?" There was still so much about him that she didn't know and that he hadn't shared.

"My mom, and she was very influential in how I was raised. At my first wedding, I incorporated a Cherokee tradition into the ceremony, for myself, as much as for my mother."

She leaned forward. He'd never mentioned that part of his wedding before. "What type of tradition?"

"We drank from a Cherokee Wedding Vase. It's a vessel that has two openings so the bride and groom can drink from it at the same time."

"That sounds lovely." It also reinforced how connected he was to his first wedding. But he'd done the best he could at their ceremony, she reminded herself. She couldn't fault him for that.

He said, "I'd considered wearing a ribbon shirt when I married Corrine because that's the traditional Cherokee wedding attire from the old days, but I went for a tux instead."

"Why?"

"Because it fit better with what she was wearing. We blended our traditions."

"Tell me more about traditional Cherokee weddings," she said, wanting to learn as much about his culture as she could. "Describe one to me."

"First off, the wedding site would be blessed for seven consecutive days. Then at the ceremony itself, the bride and groom would approach a sacred fire, each bearing gifts."

"What kind of gifts?"

"The groom would bring venison or some sort of other meat and the bride would bring corn. Those items were symbolic of him being a hunter and her tending to the farm."

"Kind of like the bow and sifter tradition?"

"Yes, it's very much like it."

"Go on, tell me the rest."

"Cherokee songs would be sung, and the bride and groom would be covered in blue blankets. After those blankets were removed, one white blanket was placed over both of them. Then, instead of exchanging rings, they exchanged the food they'd brought with them."

"That part is similar to what Ryan and Victoria did."

"In the old Paiute way, weddings weren't necessarily marked by ceremony, so Ryan incorporated some things that felt right to him. The basket they used was of Paiute origin, but it was originally made for a Navajo wedding. The Paiute have been making baskets for the Navajo for over a century."

"And the blanket?"

"I told him about Cherokee tradition, and he loosely borrowed the idea, using only one blanket instead of three."

"It's nice that you helped influence their ceremony."

"Kaley had a big hand in it, too."

"Like she did in ours."

He shrugged, smiled. "She's turning into a regular little wedding planner."

Dana smiled, too. "She's certainly good at it." She stretched out her legs. "I can't get over how pretty it is here. Look at all of the wildflowers. They're everywhere."

"Even daisies. I noticed them earlier. I should pick some for you before we go back to the house."

"That would be wonderful." She glanced at the ring he'd given her. "Daisies have become my favorite flower."

"I keep wondering if I should bring some to Corrine next time I visit her, as a gift from you." He frowned. "I'm sorry I still feel funny about you going there."

"It's okay," she said, even if it wasn't okay. It was

worse now that she loved him. "You can't help how you feel."

Torturing herself, she pressed on, wanting to know even more about his bond with Corrine. "When did you know that you loved her?"

"What do you mean?"

"Did you feel it right away? Or did it happen over time?"

"I had an immediate attraction to her when we first met. But it wasn't love at first sight. Those feelings developed as our relationship progressed."

"Do you remember the exact moment that you realized it?"

"No. But I remember that she said it first."

"Really?" Naturally, Dana was intrigued by the similarity between herself and Corrine. "She told you she loved you before you said it to her?"

"Yes, but I said it right back to her after she broke the ice. So maybe that was the moment I realized how I truly felt. Or maybe I already knew it deep inside but was waiting for her to say it first."

She looked curiously into his eyes. When she summoned the courage to tell him how she felt, would he react in the same way? Would he have a sudden revelation? Or would he pull away, leaving her wanting more?

"Will you pick those daisies for me now?" she asked, needing to feel closer to him.

"Sure." He got up and scouted around for the flowers.

He disappeared through the trees and came back with a handful of white and yellow posies. She accepted the bouquet, and when she reached forward, she felt a little flutter in her stomach.

"Oh, my God."

"What?"

"The baby moved."

"For real?" A grin split across his face.

"Yes, for real." She was grinning like a loon, too. This was the very first time she'd felt the stirrings of their child. "It was like a butterfly. Like the tiniest of wings."

He put his hand on her tummy. "I wish I could feel it."

"You will later, when it starts kicking."

"I can't wait to get home for the ultrasound. I can't wait to see who's waiting for us."

"A bow or a sifter." The appointment was less than a week away. She clutched the flowers and smiled. "I think our baby is happy that you picked these for me."

Eric leaned over to kiss her, creating more bliss. What a moment. Although Dana had already acknowledged to herself that she loved him, she realized that he was genuinely capable of making her feel loved, too.

Chapter Twelve

"It's a boy," the ultrasound technician said.

Dana's heart skipped a beat. She glanced over at Eric. He sat beside her, staring at the monitor. Staring and staring, as if he were in utter and complete awe. She'd never seen a more transfixed man.

"A son," he finally said.

"A bow," she replied. A hunter, a child who would grow up to be like his father.

"Look how amazing he is, Dana, look how much he's grown. He doesn't look like a bean anymore. He's even more perfect and beautiful than he was before." His voice vibrated. "He's everything he should be."

He absolutely was. Everything. She was overwhelmed, too. She wanted to count their son's fingers and toes and wiggle each and every one, but she couldn't do that until he was born.

Eric still hadn't quit staring. "Kaley is going to have a baby brother."

"We better start thinking up some boy's names."

"We definitely will."

They left the medical facility and went home. Eric kissed Dana with family-man intensity and headed for the nursery, determined to complete the artwork on the walls. She decided that today was the day to tell him that she loved him. It was perfect timing. She couldn't imagine a better setting or a better scenario. What could be more inspiring than your husband giving his all to the child both of you had created?

Not that she wasn't anxious about saying it. She was nervous as nervous could be. But that didn't change the fact that it needed to be said.

She waited for Eric to finish his daddy task, and when he called her into the nursery to see the outcome of his labor, she marveled at his accomplishment.

Each animal had been painted with love and care, as were the spiritual meanings that accompanied them. The brightly colored Hummingbird was Joy. The age-old Turtle represented Mother Earth. The wily-looking Coyote was a Trickster. The bold, proud Eagle reinforced Spirit. The softly painted Deer depicted Gentleness. The shiny black Raven offered Magic. The high-nosed Moose boasted Self-Esteem. Everywhere she looked, there was a wondrous animal and its Cherokee meaning.

"This is one of my totems," Eric said about Wolf.

Dana smiled. Wolf equaled Teacher. "He's definitely part of you. But so is he." She gestured to Panther because Eric reminded her of a big cat. And then she noticed that Panther represented Future.

She took a deep breath. The future. Her life with him. Their life together. This was definitely the time to tell him how she felt.

But before she could say it, he said, "Butterfly is one of your protectors, Dana."

She noticed the meaning was Transformation. "Why did you choose that for me?"

"Because when you first felt the baby move you compared it to butterfly wings. And because your body keeps changing and growing, transforming you into the mother of our child."

She smiled and spun around, making the kerchief hem of her scarf-print dress flutter.

He laughed and watched her. The sound of his laughter made her long for more and more. But she stopped before she got dizzy.

"Our son is probably seeing stars now," he said.

"I just took him to the moon."

"My wife is a moon dancer."

His wife. She liked hearing him say that. She glanced around the room and caught sight of Antelope. "I want him to protect me, too." Antelope was Action.

He cocked his head. "What's your action today? Besides taking Sweet Bean to the moon?"

Her action. Her purpose. She gazed at Antelope for support. Then she returned her attention to the man she'd married. "I've been contemplating saying this since we were in Oregon, but I've been waiting for the right time." Finally, she went ahead and did it. "I love you. I'm nervously, wonderfully in love with you, and I want you to know how I feel."

His dark skin paled, and he looked as if he couldn't

breathe. She was barely breathing, too. For the baby's sake, she forced oxygen in and out of her lungs.

"Say something, Eric."

"I don't know what to say."

"Just say anything."

He tugged a hand through his hair, spiking the short dark strands. "The only thing I can think to say is that I can't handle you loving me."

"What's wrong with a wife loving her husband? That's how life is supposed to be."

"I can't love you back, Dana."

"You can't or you won't."

"I can't."

She looked around the room for guidance and zeroed in on Elk. Its meaning was stamina. A reminder for Dana to stay strong. "You're just scared."

"Scared? I'm panicked. I appreciate that you love me. Love is one of the Creator's greatest gifts. But it isn't a gift that I can return, and that isn't fair to you."

"I'll decide what's fair to me." She glanced at Elk again. "And if I want to love my husband, then that's what I'm going to do."

"You can't fix me, Dana."

She started at his choice of words. "Who told you that I was trying to fix you?"

"No one. But that's your nature, isn't it? To make everything all right? To be perpetually positive?"

"Yes, and it's a damn good quality."

"I agree. It is. But I'm not ready for this."

"Then why do you smile so much when you're around me? And laugh? And kiss me when I need to be kissed? And hold me when I need to be held? Why do you make me feel loved if you're not ready?"

"I make you feel loved?" He took a step back. "How is that possible?"

"It's possible because you don't see yourself for who you really are."

"I know who I am. Cripes, Dana. Wake up and smell the daisies. I've been widowed for seven years and I'm still talking to my dead wife."

"I'm willing to talk to her, too."

"That's not going to do any good. She wanted me to move on. When she was dying, she begged me to find someone else someday." He made a tight face. "But I refused to listen."

"Why?"

"Why?" he mimicked, as if it was a foolish question. "Don't you get it? Don't you see? Love means loss to me."

"Yes, I get it. I've gotten it all along, but you should be focusing on how grateful you are that she loved you enough to want you to move on, rather than how much it hurt when she died."

"I don't want to have this conversation. I don't want to do this."

He walked out of the room, then out of the house. Dana stayed behind. She sat in the rocking chair in the nursery, surrounded by the Cherokee animals.

Was Eric on his way to the cemetery? She hoped that he was. She also hoped that Corrine would be able to help him this time. That somehow, she would be able to reach him, even if it was from beyond the grave.

Eric bought Corrine a bouquet of daisies similar to the ones he'd picked for Dana in the woods. In a sense, these were from her, too.

His new wife. He'd noticed how she kept looking at Elk, trying to draw upon its strength. Yet she was already strong. Dana had the spirit of a warrior. But he still didn't want her to love him. Not if he couldn't return that love.

Corrine had been just as strong as Dana. Not as wild or impulsive, but a warrior nonetheless. And where had that gotten her? Stricken with a disease that she couldn't beat.

He knelt at her grave, preparing to tell her everything that had transpired. He'd been keeping her abreast of things all along, and today he needed her more than ever.

He needed a cold white headstone?

A shiver ran through him, and he almost got up and left. But he stayed instead, doing what he always did.

He said, "We found out today that Sweet Bean is a boy. We saw him on the ultrasound, moving around in his mama's womb. He's the most beautiful kid you could imagine. When we got home from the appointment, I finished painting the nursery. I wanted to make his room as special as I could." He paused to take a hard, deep breath. "Something else happened today, too." Something he couldn't handle. "She says that she loves me, Corrine. Dana loves me."

He was met with silence. But he didn't expect an answer. These conversations were always one-sided. But they still were his lifeline to what he'd lost.

"She thinks that I behave as if I love her, too. That I laugh and smile when I'm with her, and that I hold her and kiss her when she needs it."

Were those things true? he asked himself.

He said, "She does make me laugh and smile more

than I ever have." *Ever?* Even when he'd been married to Corrine? He quickly clarified, "But she's uplifting that way. People can't help but smile and laugh around her. As for the holding and kissing when she needs it—"

He stalled, his pulse quickening. "I do it because I need it, too." Because he needed her as much she needed him, he realized. "I like having her as my wife, and I like how good we make each other feel."

He imagined that Corrine was smiling now, happy that he was admitting how successful his second marriage was.

"Don't do that," he said. "Don't make this easy on me. I shouldn't be doing this."

Doing what? his subconscious mocked. Falling in love with the woman he'd married? The fun, sweet adorable woman carrying his child? The woman who wanted nothing but the best for him?

Now what was he supposed to do? Go back and tell Dana that she was right? How was that going to help? Eric was still scared, far more troubled than when he'd first come here.

"Thanks a lot," he said to Corrine. "I'm a bigger mess than before." He scowled at the daisies and got to his feet. "I should have known that you would take her side, without any regard to how I feel. I should be the one to decide when the time is right for me to face my fears, not you or Dana or anyone else."

Frustrated, he walked to his car, and before he climbed inside, he noticed a piece of paper stuck to his shoe. He peeled it off and saw that it was a bookmark with an image of a man dressed in Biblical-era clothing holding a gold-toned pendant. The caption below the picture read, "Saint Jude, The Miracle Saint and Patron of Lost Causes."

Eric wasn't familiar with the practice of praying to saints. They weren't connected to his spiritual beliefs. Yet he slipped the bookmark into his pocket, anyway. He couldn't deny that he was feeling like a lost cause.

Or that he was in need of a miracle.

Eric went home and found Dana in the nursery, where he'd left her. She was sitting in the rocking chair, like the mama-to-be that she was.

She turned and saw him. She stood and came closer. "Did you go to see Corrine?"

"Yes."

"Do you feel better now?"

"No. Everything is worse." He was still in lost cause mode. The bookmark wasn't his miracle. It hadn't turned his feelings around. He probably should have left it for someone else to find, someone worthy of it.

"Why is everything worse?"

"Because I figured out that I'm falling in love with you, too. And I don't like it."

She merely stared at him. Then in her usual Dana way, she flashed a big bright smile. "Eventually you'll start to like it. How could you not? Being in love is miraculous."

"Yeah, and once it goes away, it's the most devastating thing in the world."

"What we have isn't going to go away. There aren't any obstacles, except your fear."

"Our age difference could be an obstacle. You're young, Dana, and there might come a time when you'll want to leave me, when I'll be too old for you."

She looked at him as if he were crazy for saying such

a thing, much less thinking it was possible. "I'm not going to outgrow my feelings for you. You need to get over the belief that love equals loss. Because I'm here to tell you that it doesn't."

"Since when were you an authority on love?"

"Since now. Since I went bonkers over you."

Did she have to be so damned sure of herself? "Fine. You love me, and I'm spiraling into that same type of feeling for you. But that doesn't give us the power to control the outcome."

"I'm not going to get sick, Eric. What happened to Corrine isn't going to happen to me."

"I didn't say you were."

"No, but we both know that's your biggest fear, and you need to stop dwelling on it."

"Easy for you to say. You don't know how it feels to watch the person you love waste away."

"No, I don't. But I know how it feels to watch my husband die while he's still alive."

Her words kicked him square in the gut. "If you got sick, Dana, I'd want to die, too."

"Oh, my beautiful man. No one is going to get sick. And no one is going to die."

"You can't make a claim like that. No one can."

"I can believe that everything will be all right. I can live by that belief."

She could. But he couldn't. "I got angry at Corrine today. It annoyed me that she was siding with you."

Dana quirked a smile. "She told you that she's on my side?"

He fought not to smile, too, or laugh, which would be worse. "Not in so many words." He deliberately frowned. "Everyone is on your side. Even Jude."

She flinched. "What?"

"St. Jude." He took the bookmark out of his pocket and handed it to her. "After I walked away from Corrine, I found this stuck to my shoe."

"Oh, this is wild. And wonderful, too." She rushed over to the table beside the rocking chair and picked up a sheet of paper. "While you were gone, I started compiling a list of names for our son. Names I was going to discuss with you." She showed it to him. "Check out the first one on the list."

He glanced down. *Jude.* He lifted his gaze to hers, his heart thumping like mad. "We're going to have to name him that now."

"I know, right?" She threw her arms around him. "It's meant to be."

He slid his hands down her spine. "What made you choose that name? What drew you to it?"

"I wanted a name that represented hope, and I started thinking about an old Beatles song that my grandmother used to play when she was feeling sad. 'Hey Jude.' The lyrics are about everything getting better. And it just seemed to fit." She held him close. "Everything is going to get better, Eric. Our little Jude is telling us that it will be. And so is Corrine. I think she made it possible for you to find the bookmark."

"But saints aren't part of my faith. Nor were they part of hers."

"That doesn't matter. It's the message that you needed to hear."

"That miracles are possible?" He nuzzled Dana's hair. "Will you go back to Corrine's grave with me? Now? Today?"

"Of course I will." She stayed warm and snug in his arms. "It would be my honor."

"I owe her an apology for getting angry."

"I'm sure she understands."

"I still need to say it. But first I need to say this to you—I love you, Dana, and I'm going to do whatever I can to make miracles with you."

And keep making them for the rest of their lives.

Immersed in the comfort of her husband, Dana accompanied him to the cemetery. As soon as she saw the bouquet of flowers he'd left earlier, she smiled.

"You brought her daisies."

"It just seemed like what I was supposed to do."

"They're beautiful."

"I intended for them to be from you, too."

"Thank you. You know how much that matters to me."

"Next time we can pick something from the garden."

"That would be nice." But this was nice, too. Following his lead, she knelt beside the grave.

"How does it feel to have your first experience like this?" he asked.

Her first time at a cemetery. "It's humbling." A reminder of how fragile humanity was, and how important being happy was, too. "We're all going to die someday. But it's how we value life that's important. And how we live it."

"Corrine lived hers with hope and joy."

"She must have been a very special lady."

"She was. You can introduce yourself, if you want to. Unless that's seems strange to you."

"It's not strange." It seemed to make sense, especially after all this time of wanting to come here. She put her hand on top of the headstone and said, "I'm Dana. I'm Eric's new wife. The one he's been telling you about." She moved her hand to her stomach. "And this is Jude. We just named him that today. A name you helped inspire."

Eric spoke next, "I'm sorry, Corrine, for getting mad at you earlier. You were right to tell me that I should move on with my life after you were gone. You loved me enough to try to release me from my grief. But I refused to listen until today."

Dana softly interjected, "After Jude is born we'll bring him here so you can meet him. And we'll bring Kaley with us, too. We'll come here as a family."

"A happy family," Eric added.

She glanced over at him and smiled. Then she said to Corrine, "I love Eric. I love him as much as you did, and I know that I have your blessing. Not just because you encouraged him to find someone else someday, but because you made yourself known when we both needed you."

"She'll always be here," Eric said.

"Yes, she will." Always in the wind, always in his heart.

Only now, Dana's husband was ready to live once again.

Chapter Thirteen

Dana's pregnancy progressed as it should, and on the day of her baby shower, she laughed and talked and ate. Surrounded by helium-filled balloons and animal-print decorations, she opened presents. She even felt Jude kicking away in her belly. But he kicked all the time now. He poked his little feet out. Sometimes he elbowed her, too. Eric, of course, loved how strong and persistent their son was. Kaley was also thrilled by her baby brother's tenacious manner.

"Jude is going to be hell on wheels," she told the other women at the shower. "He's going to rule this house."

"I'll bet you were a tough little cookie, too," Dana said.

"I can vouch for how much she kicked," Victoria said. "Bang, bang, bang in my belly. Just when I'd try to sleep, there went Kaley, jamming her high heels into my ribs."

The teenager laughed. "I wasn't wearing heels then."

"It sure felt like it."

Dana watched the exchange. It was nice that Victoria had flown in for the shower. And it was even nicer that she was able to talk about her pregnancy with sweetness and humor, sharing those moments with her daughter.

Dana was going to do the same thing with Jude someday, although she wondered if a boy would care quite as much. Maybe when he was older and starting a family of his own, he would be interested in these types of stories.

It was strange to be thinking about the faraway future in such a vivid way. Dana had always been a live-for-the-day person, but now that she was having a child, she was considering every aspect of his life, as well as the rest of the family's.

"All I know," she said, "is how much Kaley is going to spoil her brother. Look at all these gifts." Many of them had come from Kaley. She'd obviously gone on a madly happy shopping spree. But Dana was certain that Kaley was going to spoil Jude in other ways, too.

"Just think of how many built-in babysitters you'll have." This from Candy. "Me included."

"Ah, yes. My BFF and Jude's future godmother." As wonderful as this shower was, Dana couldn't help but feel for Candy. Here was a woman who'd lost her baby and the joy that went with it. "Where would I be without you?"

Candy grinned. "Still fretting over the pregnancy test?"

Dana grinned, too, grateful as always that Candy was

going to play such a loving role in her son's life. She was the sister Dana never had. How fortunate she was to have met Candy when she did. Dana was blessed in every way imaginable.

Victoria lifted a baby outfit off the coffee table. "Look how tiny and adorable this is. A plaid shirt with diaper snaps."

"Doesn't it make you want one?" Kaley asked her.

"I don't think it would fit me," her birth mother replied.

"I was talking about another kid." Kaley struck a pretty pose. "Another version of me, only smaller." She teasingly added, "And one you get to keep this time."

Victoria laughed. "Believe me, my darling, I knew what you meant. And yes, it makes me want one. But I'm trying to contain myself."

"You have my permission," Kaley said.

"Mine, too," Dana added. "You and Ryan are going to have to get cracking."

"We will. In due time." Victoria reached for another of Jude's outfits. "But for now, I'm just going to delight in all of this."

Dana was delighting in it, too. "Check out the baseball uniform. And the bib overalls and the skinny jeans for when he's a little older. Who knew boys' clothes could be so cool?"

Kaley said to Victoria, "When you do decide the time is right, maybe you'll have a boy, too. Then I'll have two little brothers, and they can be bestie cousins."

"That would be cute." Her birth mother made a wistful expression.

Was the idea of having a baby sooner than later starting to grow on her? Or was she just caught up in the moment?

"You're not getting any younger," Kaley said to her.

Victoria snapped a balloon in her daughter's direction. "Quit trying to con me."

"She's good at it," Dana said. Kaley was a master at persuasion.

"She's good at everything," Victoria replied. "Maybe I'll have another girl just like her."

Other guests jumped into the conversation, and the discussion turned to the differences between raising girls and boys. A lot of the women in attendance had kids, so Dana listened to them talk about their children, pride alive in their voices.

Nothing was going to compare to being a parent, and she couldn't wait for Jude to be born.

Later that day, after the guests were gone and everything was cleaned up, Eric returned home. Dana led him into the nursery where she'd laid out the presents.

"Dang," he said, "our kid scored."

"A lot of it is from Kaley, but everyone else was generous, as well."

"I expected Kaley and Victoria to still be here."

"They went to Kaley's dorm. They wanted to spend some time alone together before Victoria goes back to Oregon."

"That's understandable." He came forward to hug her, and they both laughed when her belly got in the way. Then she sighed from the nearness of him.

"You're such the ultimate husband," she said, expressing her joy of being in his arms.

"I wasn't so ultimate in the beginning. I was a wreck at our wedding."

"You're the proud groom now. You carry around a wedding picture of us in your wallet, and our photo album is prominently displayed in the living room."

"I know, but I still regret that I stumbled through one of the most important days of our lives. Maybe next year we can have an anniversary party to make up for it."

"That sounds wonderful." She gave him a cozy kiss. "But at the moment, I'm partied out." Although she'd enjoyed every minute of her shower, she was ready to unwind.

"Yeah, I'll bet. You and Jude have had quite a day."

"You wouldn't believe how much cake I ate. Do you want a piece? There's a half sheet leftover."

"What kind is it?"

"Chocolate with chocolate cream filling and white icing. It's really, really good. And fun, too. It's decorated with little sugar zoo animals. They were almost too cute to eat."

He smiled. "Almost, huh?"

"Jude wanted to try them."

"Then his daddy will, too."

They proceeded to the kitchen and he cut himself a big slice and poured a glass of milk to go with it. Dana watched him eat. Then she stuck her finger into the filling and scooped up a glob of it.

"Hey." He pretended to shield his plate. "You already had yours."

"Jude wants to tastes yours."

"Listen to you. Blaming it on our son."

"What can I say? He's going to be a chocolate hound."

"You're the chocolate hound, Mrs. Reeves."

"That's Mrs. Cherry Reeves to you," she replied,

reminding him about her Cherry nickname from their honeymoon night. "Seriously, though, can you believe how far we've come in such a short amount of time?"

He leaned over to whisper in her ear. "Life is good. Love is good." He nibbled on her lobe. "This cake is damned good, too."

She erupted into a silly giggle. "I told you."

"And you were right. But you've been right about everything all along."

She considered what he said. "Actually, I wasn't. I was wrong to think that I could fix you. People can't fix each other. Each of us is responsible for ourselves."

"That's true. But you helped me see the light. You were there when I needed you, showing me the way. You might be young, Dana, but you have the soul of a wise old owl."

"Does that mean that we're going to age at the same rate now?"

"In a spiritual sense, I would say so. In a physical sense, you're still going to be pushing me around in a wheelchair someday."

She nudged him under the table. His old-man jokes didn't concern her anymore. These days, Eric had the youth and vitality of a man half his age. He'd come a long way, making strides in every direction.

After he finished the cake, he said, "Want to help me eat another piece?"

"Sure."

"I figured as much." He cut another slice, even bigger this time. He handed her a fork, and they shared it from the same plate, attacking the little sugar animals.

She said, "Remember what you told me about zebras?"

"About how they imprint with their young?"

She nodded. "It started to make me wonder about other types of animals and how they care for their offspring. I even did a little research."

"What did you find out?"

"Tons of stuff. Like baby elephants weigh about two-hundred-and-fifty pounds when they're born. And soon afterward, the mother selects several full-time babysitters from her group to watch over her baby when the herd travels."

He chuckled. "If I had a two-hundred-and-fifty pound kid, I'd be looking for babysitters, too."

She rolled her eyes, but she laughed, too. "Baby elephants don't have very good survival skills, so I guess they need extra keepers."

"What other animals did you research?"

"The usual." She tossed a bit of wit at him. "Lions and tigers and bears." She waited for him to say, "Oh, my," which he did, and they laughed again.

They also went to town on the cake, enjoying voracious bites. They shared the milk, too, refilling the glass.

She said, "I really did look up lions and tigers and bears and discovered things they had in common."

He glanced up from his fork. "Like what?"

"All of them are born blind and are completely reliant on their mothers. Plus newborn bears are even toothless and bald."

"Poor babies."

"I know. They're so sweet and helpless, and then they grow up to be so big and fierce."

"And beautiful."

She agreed. All of those animals were beautiful. "I

read about fawns, too." She thought about the gentle depiction of the deer painted on Jude's wall. "In the first few minutes of a fawn's life, the mother licks it clean, removing its scent to keep the predators away. Then she keeps it hidden in the grass for a week until it's strong enough to walk with her."

"It's nice how you're preparing for motherhood by learning about other creatures." He looked at her as if she was a delicate creature herself. "Did you study penguins?"

She nodded. "The parents work together to care for their young. After the nesting period, the little penguins are sometimes grouped in nurseries with other baby penguins while their parents hunt for food." She paused to consider the information she'd gathered. "I also read that some types of penguins mate for life and others only mate for a season."

"I've always found that sort of thing fascinating. Which animals stay together and which don't."

"Me, too. Especially since some humans stay together and some don't."

"It's different with our species, though. If we mate for life, it's because we choose to, not because it's part of our science."

"Our emotions drive us."

"Boy, do they ever."

They gazed silently at each other. Their emotions were driving them right now.

"You've done this twice," she said.

"Decided that someone was my lifelong partner?"

"Yes." Only Corrine's life had been cut short, but that went without saying.

"I've been lucky to have found this kind of love with two different women."

"And I'm lucky that I found it with you."

They went silent again, steeped in the moment. She moved her chair closer to his and he kissed her. He tasted like chocolate cream, but she probably did, too. It was a dreamy, sexy flavor. She moaned her pleasure.

"Touch me," she said.

"I am touching you."

"Touch me some more."

He nuzzled her cheek. "Are you propositioning me? In your condition?"

"Yes, and you better take me up on my offer before my belly gets any bigger."

"Is it getting bigger as we speak?"

"Probably."

"Then we better hurry." He kissed her again, but he didn't hurry. He took his sweet, sensual time.

Finally, they went into the bedroom, and with the blinds closed and a single candle burning, they stepped out of their shoes and removed each other's clothes. That was another slow process. But the results were worth it.

"Who knew a pregnant woman could be so seductive?" He ran his hands along her naked body and when he reached her belly, he caressed it with warmth and care.

She caressed him, as well. The breadth of his shoulders, the flatness of his stomach. He was a male in his prime, and he was deliciously aroused. She stroked him there, too.

He sucked in his breath. "You're wicked."

"So are you." Gently wicked.

They got into bed, pleasuring each other with familiarity. That was part of the beauty of having a mate. They knew how to make each other feel good.

He entered her, and they made love in a position that had become natural during her pregnancy. She floated on the feeling, on the desire.

"Thank you for being my wife," he said, the romantic impact of his words shimmying down her spine.

"I wouldn't have it any other way." She had everything she ever needed or wanted, and she loved the man she'd married, more and more with each day.

Time passed quickly, so quickly that Dana's due date had come and gone before she knew it. As of yesterday, Jude was late. But the doctor told them not to worry. If the pregnancy lasted for longer than forty-two weeks, he would induce labor. For now, it wasn't necessary. Most likely, Jude would be rolling into the world any day.

Eric couldn't wait to meet his son in person, to hold him, to watch him nap, to see him nurse from his mama. He was even looking forward to changing diapers. All he wanted was for Jude to make his much-anticipated appearance.

Tonight Eric was sitting in the living room, watching TV. Dana had turned in early. She was just as anxious for Jude to be born as he was. But apparently the kid was enjoying driving his parents nuts. His sister, too. Kaley called incessantly, asking for news. Eric assured her she would be notified as soon as Dana went into labor.

Eric switched channels on the remote. He couldn't seem to concentrate on any of the shows. Finally, he gave up and went into the bedroom to check on Dana. She was sound asleep. Although he had the husbandly urge to stroke her hair and move it away from her face, he let her be. If he woke her up, she might struggle to go back to sleep, and she needed her rest.

To keep himself occupied, he went onto the patio and turned on the lights. The garden he and Dana had planted was flourishing, and it gave him peace to look at it. Mostly it was filled with winter flowers now. Pansies, sweet alyssum and pinks grew in abundance, making a colorful and fragrant display. The pinks were his favorite, a type of carnation with serrated edges that looked as if they'd been cut with pinking shears—hence the name. He'd learned details about them from Dana. He'd learned a lot from his young wife.

A short while later, Eric headed for the nursery and gazed at the animals. He was certain that each and every one of them was going to protect the baby. He believed that St. Jude was part of the deal, too. They had lovingly framed the bookmark and hung it on the wall.

The crib had been ready for what seemed like forever, made up with soft blue sheets and a fluffy comforter. Everything was ready for Jude's arrival. The dresser contained his sleepers and the changing table was stocked with diapers and lotion and powder. Even his car seat and stroller waited idly by. So did an infant swing that Eric had put together just this week. He walked over to it and turned it on, imagining Jude rocking inside it, drifting into a sweet abyss.

He recalled feeling this way when he and Corrine had prepared for Kaley. Only they'd been scared at times, hoping and praying that the birth mother didn't change her mind and keep the baby. Adoption was frightening in that way.

But it had worked out beautifully, right up to Kaley's relationship with Ryan and Victoria now.

He shut down the nursery and joined his wife in bed, cautious not to disturb her.

In the morning, she woke him up with a quick shake and a big grin, "Guess what, papa? My water broke."

He sat up so fast, the room nearly spun. "Did you call the doctor?"

She nodded. "We need to go to the hospital."

The hospital. Yes. He knew that. He jumped out of bed and threw on his clothes. Dana looked far too calm for a woman who was having a baby. She was already ready to leave the house. She'd even changed into a dry dress, a yellow cotton frock with heart-shaped buttons. She was like the sun on a magical day, with her cheery outfit and hair in a ponytail.

Eric tried to stay calm, too, but he was just so darn nervous. Jude was on his way. "Have you had any contractions yet?"

"No, but for some women the pain doesn't start right away. It could be up to an hour before it happens."

He hoped that was how it happened for her. They would be at the hospital way before then.

He helped her into the car, put her prepacked bag in the trunk and backed out of the driveway. On the main highway, they got caught in traffic.

He said, "I always figured we'd be doing this in the middle of the night."

"Instead of during everyone else's work commute? Don't worry about it, Eric. We'll get there." She laughed a little. "You're gripping the steering wheel like an old man."

"I am an old man, and I have precious cargo on board." When they stopped at a red light, he reached for her hand. "I love you, Dana."

She graced him with a smile. "I love you, too."

"I wish the hospital was closer."

"It's not that far."

"It's far enough." Especially since some of the other drivers weren't focused on the road. The guy behind them was drinking what appeared to be takeout coffee and the woman next to them looked as if she might be sneaking in a text. All Eric wanted to do was get to their destination.

The light changed and he crossed the intersection. The next light they came to was yellow. Eric slowed down, preparing to stop.

Then suddenly...

Boom!

Coffee Guy didn't hit his breaks in time and rammed straight into the back of Eric and Dana's car. The impact wasn't strong enough to deploy the airbags, but it was still a whiplash-type jolt and the most frightening moment of Eric's life.

He quickly looked over at Dana.

"I'm all right," she said.

Was she? She looked pale and frightened, too.

Behind them, Coffee Guy was motioning to pull over to the side of the road to exchange insurance information, obviously trying to do the right thing.

Eric waved him away. They didn't have time for that. He looked at Dana again, and she was even paler than before and making a terrible face.

"You're not all right," he said, his heart lodging in his throat.

"Yes, I am. It's just that I think the accident triggered my labor. Or maybe my pains would have started, anyway."

"I should forget trying to get you to the hospital myself and call an ambulance."

"Really, I'm okay."

"I'm calling for help." He pulled over. Coffee Guy pulled over, as well, probably assuming that Eric had changed his mind about exchanging information.

"This isn't necessary," Dana said.

"Yes, it is." He dialed 9-1-1 and told them that he and his pregnant wife were on the way to the hospital and had been in an accident. He explained that her water had already broken and that—

She was bleeding. Somewhere between the beginning of the phone call and her telling him that she was okay, she'd begun to bleed. Bright red all over her yellow dress.

Panicked, he screamed into the phone. Dana was doubled over in pain. By this time, Coffee Guy was standing at the driver's side window, staring in at them.

Eric reached for his wife and held on to her shoulders. She buried her face against his neck, and in a raspy, pain-induced voice, she told him, "We're going to make it. We will, I promise."

We. Her and Jude.

"Of course you will," he replied, so damned afraid that they were going to die.

Dana didn't speak after that. She was too weak to talk.

The ambulance arrived quickly. Eric hadn't quit shaking. He rode with Dana while the MTs treated her. She was losing too much blood and needed a transfusion. Her vital signs were weak. The baby was in distress, too. The love of Eric's life was fading away and so was their son.

Chapter Fourteen

At the hospital Dana was rushed into emergency surgery and Eric was left to wait. Trauma from the accident had caused placental abruption, where the placenta had separated from the womb.

Numb, he stared at the walls. Then he thought about Kaley. He was supposed to call her when Dana went into labor. But how could he call his precious daughter and tell her that Dana and Jude were fighting for their lives?

Eric wanted to curse the Creator. He wanted to curse the man who'd been drinking his stupid coffee. He wanted to curse the entire world and everyone in it.

He couldn't do this again. He couldn't lose another wife. Or a child. Or anyone else he loved.

But he wasn't going to lose them, he told himself. Dana had promised him that she and Jude would make it. She'd clung to him and promised, and he had to believe her. He *had* to.

Instead of cursing anyone, Eric said a Cherokee prayer. He spoke to St. Jude, too. He even called upon the animals that protected Dana and Jude. And lastly, he asked Corrine to help if she could.

Finally, he summoned the strength to call Kaley and relay the news.

"I'll be there as soon as I can," she said, her voice quavering. "And I'll call Candy. She'll want to be there, too."

Kaley and Candy arrived at nearly the same time. Kaley rushed into his arms and burst into tears. He stroked a hand down her hair.

"It will be okay," he told her.

"Mom used to say that."

"I know. But this time, it will be."

"Aren't you scared, Dad?"

"I'm petrified, baby girl. But I can't let that fear control me. Dana wouldn't want me to." He looked past Kaley and met Candy's gaze. She looked like a lost soul, too.

Eric was the strongest of all of them. But that was his role as a man, as a husband and father, as the head of the family. He had to stay strong for everyone, including himself.

He released Kaley and hugged Candy. Afterward the three of them sat side by side. Time ticked by. Kaley kept tearing up. His daughter wasn't doing well.

She said to Candy, "I hated hospitals after my mom died. She passed away in a cancer ward, and I only associated hospitals with pain. Then I met my birth parents and discovered that Victoria had a bad experience with hospitals, too." Kaley explained what Candy probably already knew. "When I was born, Ryan never came to see her like he was supposed to, and all she remembered was me being taken away by the adoption agency and her being alone." The teen continued, "So when I was in Oregon the first time, I suggested that Ryan and Victoria take me to the hospital where I was born so we could all have a new experience."

"Did it help?" Candy asked.

"Yes. It did. But now this reminds me of when Mom died." She glanced over at Eric. She was tearing up again. "I'm so sorry, Dad. I'm really trying to not feel that way."

He put his arm around her. He knew she was struggling to be brave. "You don't have to wait around here if you can't handle it. I'll call you when we hear something."

"Oh, no. I could never leave. Never. I just wished they would hurry up. I want to see Dana and my brother. I want them to be all right."

Suddenly an image of Dana in the car flashed in Eric's mind. Holding her while she shivered, her body contorting in pain, the blood soaking the front of her dress.

He closed his eyes, but the crimson stain wouldn't go away. What if she didn't survive? What if he lost Dana? And what if little Jude perished with her?

"Does anyone want coffee?" Candy asked.

Eric opened his eyes, his breath catching hard and quick. But the images just kept coming. Coffee Guy ramming his car into them. Coffee Guy staring at Dana in horror. Candy and Kaley didn't know the details of the accident, and Eric couldn't bear to tell them.

"Nothing for me," he said. His strength was faltering,

like Samson getting his hair shorn. Eric even dragged a hand through his own hair.

"I'll take a cup of hot chocolate," Kaley said.

"I'll get it for you." Candy headed for the nearest vending machine, obviously needing to be useful.

Kaley said, "I wish I could control my fear, Dad. I wish I could be more like you."

He pulled himself together. No more blood-soaked images. No more what-ifs. His daughter was counting on him for hope. True, heartfelt hope. "I grieved too long and too hard for your mom. I grieved before she was even gone, refusing to listen when she encouraged me to love someone else someday. And now that I do love someone else, I'm not giving up. And neither are you. We'll hang on together, like a family should."

"I love you, Daddy."

"I love you, too. You're my grown-up girl." A beautiful young woman with a beautiful life ahead of her. "You convinced me that I was meant to marry Dana and have a child with her. You helped me come to terms with the past and embrace my future with you and Dana and baby Jude."

Candy returned with Kaley's hot chocolate. Then she said to Eric, "Are you sure I can't get you anything?"

"Actually, if you don't mind, I'll take that coffee now. Cream, no sugar."

"Coming right up." Once again, Candy seemed grateful to keep busy.

After she brought Eric his coffee, he thanked her and she resumed her seat. He took a sip and thought about all of the wonderful things he and Dana had shared so far. He made damned sure that this coffee, the one he was drinking now, and every cup thereafter, would be associated with love and happiness.

He wasn't going to let anything stand in the way of his belief that Dana and Jude would be coming home to him.

"I'll be right back," he told Kaley and Candy.

Eric took the elevator to the first floor, where the gift shop was, hoping to find items that were meaningful. Mostly they had flowers, balloons, stuffed toys and books, but he also noticed a small case of fourteen-carat gold jewelry.

He bought a bracelet for his wife, with a "Mom" charm to go with it. He purchased the same bracelet for Kaley and Candy, but with different charms. Kaley's said "Sister" and Candy's said "Friend." For Jude he found a dolphin-shaped nightlight for the nursery.

He went back to the waiting area and gave Kaley and Candy their bracelets. Both women got teary-eyed, particularly when he showed them Dana's.

"As soon as they let me see her," he said, "I'm going to put it on her wrist." He removed the nightlight from the bag. "And this is for the baby's room."

"That's perfect, Dad." Kaley leaned against his shoulder, then told Candy, "In Cherokee tradition, dolphin represents the sacredness of life."

Candy reached for the nightlight and examined the design. "It's beautiful. And very fitting." She returned it to Eric.

He took the dolphin and tucked it back into the bag, with the old adage "Where there's life, there's hope" swirling in his mind.

Dana's doctor, still dressed in his scrubs, appeared in the distance, and Eric and the girls jumped up. But then Kaley stalled, obviously afraid to move forward.

Eric remembered how desperately she'd cried when her mother had died. That picture of his sweet little eleven-year-old daughter would be forever embedded in his mind. Her grief. Her pain.

He took her hand, showing her the way. The surgeon was coming toward them with a confident stride. The news had to be good.

The news was wonderful. There were no further complications. Dana was doing well and so was the baby. She was in recovery and Jude was in the nursery. Later, both mother and child would be taken to a semi-private room. "The baby," the doctor added with a smile, "is already the apple of his mother's eye. She can't quit talking about him. And he's a big one. Nine pounds, six ounces. You've got yourself a strong, healthy son."

Eric thanked the doctor with a handshake. He also thanked the Creator for answering his prayers.

While Kaley and Candy darted over to the nursery, Eric was ushered into the recovery room to see Dana.

It was a quiet area with patients resting in gurneys, each separated by a curtain. Dana was at the end of the row. He approached her with his heart in his hands. He loved her more than ever.

She looked exhausted from her ordeal, with shadows beneath her eyes and an IV drip attached to her arm. But to him, she was the most beautiful woman on earth. He sat beside her gurney, and she turned her head toward him. She smiled groggily and said, "Have you seen Jude?"

"Not yet. But I will just as soon I spend a few minutes with you. Kaley and Candy are at the nursery now, cooing over him, I'm sure."

"He's gorgeous. He looks like you, Eric. And like me, too. I'm so enamored with him. I can't wait until I can hold him and never let go."

He stroked her cheek, so damned grateful to be able to touch her. "Me, too."

"I won't be able to lift him right away because of the surgery. But I can still nurse him, as long as someone puts him in my arms. They assured me that my milk wouldn't be affected by the medications they gave me."

"I'll put him in your arms. I'll be there whenever you need me." He reached for her hand. He loved her so much.

After a reflective moment, he added, "I stayed positive while you were in surgery. I followed your lead and believed that everything was going to be okay. I tried to keep Kaley and Candy from breaking down, too."

"You're my hero."

And she was his. "I learned from the best." He slipped the bracelet he'd bought her around her wrist and latched it. "It's a charm bracelet that says 'Mom.' I bought it in the gift shop here at the hospital." He told her about the matching jewelry he'd found for Kaley and Candy. He also showed her the nightlight for the baby's room and explained the significance of it.

She touched the dolphin. "Now Jude has another protector. One that will shine for him at night." She looked up at him. "Thank you for being my husband and for giving me a child."

"I should be the one thanking you." He kissed her, skimming his lips across hers and marveling in the warmth and softness. He could have kissed her for an eternity. "Rest well, and I'll see you in your room later."

She smiled her beautiful smile. "Go meet your son, Eric."

"I'm on my way." He kissed her again and whispered a soft, loving goodbye.

He took the corridor to the nursery and spotted Kaley and Candy at the glass window. Kaley waved him over.

"How's Dana?" she quickly asked.

"She's doing fine, and she wants me to meet my son."

"There he is, Dad." She proudly pointed to an infant in the front row.

Jude lay swaddled in a blue blanket in a clear bassinet. He had a cap of dark hair and a sweet little face.

Eric just stood there, staring at him, the way he'd stared at the monitor screen when he'd seen the baby inside Dana's womb on the ultrasound.

Only he was here now, right here, on the other side of the glass. Eric lifted his hands and pressed both palms against the barrier. He understood what Dana meant about wanting to hold the baby and never let go.

Candy motioned to the nurse who was caring for the infants, letting her know that Jude's daddy was here.

The nurse picked up the baby and brought him closer so Eric could get a better look at him.

"Isn't he cool?" Kaley said.

"Yeah." Eric grinned. "He's the coolest."

"Congratulations," Candy said.

"Thank you." He noticed that both she and Kaley had tears in their eyes. So did he, and Eric wasn't prone to crying. But they were happy tears, and that was all that mattered.

The nurse put Jude back in his bassinette, and Eric imagined how warm and cozy the baby was going to feel in his arms.

He said to Kaley, "This is like when you first came into my life. The same overwhelming joy of becoming a parent."

She leaned against his shoulder. "It's the same feeling for me, only it's the overwhelming joy of becoming a big sister."

He put his arm around his daughter. "It's such an immediate love."

"That's how family love is supposed to be." She went philosophical. "This makes me appreciate how hard it was for Victoria to give me up after I was born, and how tough it was on Ryan for what he did, too. I understood it before, but I really understand it now."

"You should call and let them know that Jude is here."

"I'll call right now." She walked away and found a waiting room where she could sit and talk.

Candy moved to stand beside Eric, and he turned toward her. "You've been an amazing friend to my wife," he said.

"She's an amazing woman."

"So are you." He thought about her divorce and the baby she'd lost. "I never believed that I would find love and happiness again. But I did, and I hope you do, too."

"Thank you. But I'm not ready to start over just yet."

"I didn't think I was ready, either."

"I'll keep that in mind if I ever meet anyone. But for now, just being Jude's godmother is enough."

"Dana couldn't have chosen a better person for that role."

"I'm honored to be part of your son's life, Eric. He's a lucky little boy to have you and Dana as his parents."

"We're lucky to have him. If he hadn't been conceived, Dana and I wouldn't have gotten married. He brought us together." He laughed a little. "Him and Kaley. She was pretty persistent about the marriage."

"You raised a strong-willed daughter. But she was falling apart when Dana was in surgery. So was I. It was just so difficult to bear the thought of something tragic happening."

"That's why I knew I couldn't lose hope." He turned to look at Jude again, to admire the baby he and Dana had created.

"Did you call Dana's mother and grandmother? Do they know anything about what happened today?" Candy asked.

"Not yet." He'd made a conscious choice not to call until Dana and Jude were out of danger. "I didn't want to worry them, especially since they're so far away. I wanted to wait until I got word that Dana and Jude were okay."

"I can call them now if you'd like. I have their number programmed into my phone."

"That would be great." If Candy wanted to do the honor, he would let her. "Tell them I'll talk to them in a few hours and let them know what room Dana is in once she's out of recovery. And tell them how spectacular Jude is."

"Believe me, I will. I'll go meet up with Kaley and do it now."

Candy walked away, leaving Eric alone at the nursery window with his son, a baby whose name was associated with miracles.

Dana watched her husband cradle their child in his arms. She was in her room now, with her family by her side, including Candy. At this point, Candy was as close to family as a friend could get and Dana would always see her that way.

Dana was surrounded by love. With Eric's help, she'd already nursed the baby. She'd held Jude so close that while he'd suckled she'd wanted to burst with the joy of it.

"He does look like both of us," Eric said. "He has my coloring and your bright blue eyes."

"He's going to be quite the ladies' man," Candy said.

"Yep." Kaley grinned from her chair. She'd already taken tons of pictures of the baby with her smartphone and texted the images to everyone in her contacts list. Her phone had been beeping like crazy with responses.

Candy came over and sat beside Dana. "How are you holding up?"

"I'm tired, but I've never been happier." She glanced over at Eric again. He was walking the baby around the room.

"You picked a good one, that's for sure."

She nodded. She knew Candy was talking about Eric. "I can't wait until Jude and I can go home with him."

"How long will that be?"

"I'm not sure. Three or four days, maybe."

"Just rest while you're here."

"I will. I want to get better." She took yet another glance at her husband. She couldn't seem to stop looking at him. "He already arranged to take time off from work to help me with the baby. And now that I had surgery, I'm going to value his help more than ever."

"I'll come by when I can. And so will Kaley." Candy leaned in close. "You'd be proud of the way Eric kept us together while you were in surgery."

"He told me that he stayed positive for everyone." And it made her heart glad to hear it from Candy. She would never tire of knowing that Eric had truly conquered his fears.

Suddenly he looked over and smiled. Both women returned his smile. The baby had fallen asleep in his arms.

"Can I hold him?" Kaley asked.

"Sure." Eric approached his daughter.

She turned off her phone and put it away. He transferred the infant into her waiting arms.

"Hey, Jude," she said, quite purposefully. "We're going to be saying that a lot of him." She sang the first few lines of the song. "I downloaded it so I would know the words."

"I'm sure he appreciates it," Dana told her.

Kaley rocked the baby. "He seems to. Look at his little face. It's so scrunched up."

Eric laughed. "Yours was like that, too."

"I know. It's amazing how beautiful newborns are, even with those funny little faces."

Dana said, "I think it's those funny little faces that make them beautiful."

Candy resumed the chair beside Kaley's, leaving the bed free for Eric. He scooted in next to Dana and they held hands, content in the closeness.

Kaley brought Jude over to Dana and placed the baby in her arms, giving her a chance to hold her son again. Eric stroked the baby's hair and Jude opened his eyes and squinted at his parents. They smiled, awed by the moment.

And every moment that was yet to come.

Epilogue

Eric watched Dana bustle around the diner. He'd come here for dinner with Jude. Their one-year-old son sat in a high chair, playing with a plastic truck and grinning his adorable grin. His blue eyes sparkled every time he caught sight of his mother.

Dana worked here a few days a week, and although she was still in school, she kept changing her mind about her major. She wasn't sure if she wanted to be an interior designer. She was considering psychology or animal husbandry or heaven knew what else. She was as beautifully scattered as ever. But she was also the best wife and mother in the world. Eric thanked the Creator every day for her.

Jude banged his toy on the high chair tray and said, "Mama."

"I know, little man. Your mama is working tonight.

But she'll be off soon and she's going to sit down and eat with us. She put in a food order for herself, too."

As promised, Dana finished up with her other customers, then joined Eric and Jude. She set their meals on the table and kissed the top of Jude's head. He showed her his toy, and she kissed it, too. The boy laughed and handed it to Eric.

"Dada," he said.

Eric took the truck and mimicked Dana, kissing the wheels of the vehicle. Jude laughed again, and Eric returned the toy.

"Eat your dinner, sweetie." Dana adjusted the child's bib and motioned to the finger food she'd placed on his tray.

He squished most of it, but he nibbled on some, too.

She sat across from Eric. "Hello, lover."

"Hello to you." He smiled. She looked like a dream, in her bright pink uniform with a silk flower in her hair. He enjoyed seeing her in her work clothes. It was a reminder of how they'd met.

"Meat loaf for my husband." She motioned for him to eat, with the same waggling-finger wave that she'd given to their son.

He looked at her plate. She was having spaghetti and meatballs. "If Jude decides he wants some of that, it's going to create a mess."

She shrugged. "I brought plenty of napkins. And we've got baby wipes in the diaper bag."

As always, nothing fazed Dana. He loved that about her. Eric imagined spaghetti in the kid's hair.

The miracle kid, he thought.

He looked over at Jude. He was pouring water from his sippy cup onto his food in typical toddler fashion.

"We should have another one," Dana said.

Eric just stared at her. "Another baby?"

She laughed. "Yes, but I was just kidding. I wanted to see the panic on your face."

"Are you sure you're not hankering for another one?"

"I'm positive. Our little guy is enough for me."

By now Jude was running his truck through the food. Eric chuckled. "For me, too."

"Ryan and Victoria are finally trying for a baby."

"They are? How do you know that?"

"Victoria told Kaley, and Kaley told me."

"Ah, the women's circle. Talk. Talk. Talk." When she raised her eyebrows at him, he quickly added, "That's great about Ryan and Victoria. I hope it happens soon for them."

"It probably will. Look how easily they conceived Kaley."

She twined a glob of spaghetti around her fork. "Things aren't going so well for Candy, though. She's going to have to sell her house."

"Really? Why?"

"She owed a balloon payment and it came due, and now she doesn't have the money. She tried to refinance, but she's in over her head and can't get another loan. She's going to try to sell the house herself instead of using a Realtor because she can't afford to give away the commission."

"I'm sorry that she's in trouble. I wish I had the money to loan her."

"Oh, that's nice of you to want to help. But she'll get through it. And who knows, maybe something really good will come of it."

Eric didn't see where anything good was going to

come out of being forced to sell your house, but he knew better than to question Dana's positive beliefs. She'd been right so far.

He cut into his meat loaf. "You know what's weird? I actually know someone who's looking to buy a house in her area."

Her eyes lit up. "Who?"

"An old powwow friend of mine. You haven't met him yet. I just ran into him the other day and while we were catching up, he mentioned that he was house-hunting."

"You should put him in touch with Candy."

"I will, but there's no guarantee that a sale will be made between them."

"It seems kind of fate-ish, though, don't you think?"

"What does? Me knowing someone who's looking for a house at the same time she's selling hers? I suppose it does, but not everything is fate. It could just be coincidence."

"I don't believe in coincidence. Everything happens for a reason." She turned to Jude. "Right, baby?"

The boy banged his toy in the mess he'd made, splashing himself and Dana. She laughed and cupped his food-splattered cheeks. He tried to reach for her spaghetti.

Here it comes, Eric thought. The bigger mess. The mother-and-son chaos. Jude had his mama's free-spirited personality.

"You want some?" She fed him from her fork. But that only lasted for a few bites.

Within no time, Jude was squeezing bits of pasta between his fingers and pealing into happy hysterics, right along with Dana.

Eric removed the baby wipes from the diaper bag, preparing to tackle the mess when it was over. But he laughed, too. How could he not? His family always gave him insurmountable joy. They were his life, his love, his never-ending bliss.

He wouldn't trade their nuttiness for all of the normalcy in the world. Eric liked things just the way they were.

* * * * *

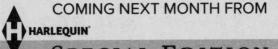

COMING NEXT MONTH FROM

SPECIAL EDITION

Available October 22, 2013

#2293 A MAVERICK UNDER THE MISTLETOE
Montana Mavericks: Rust Creek Cowboys
by Brenda Harlen
When Sutter Traub had a falling-out with his family, he took off to Seattle. But now he's back—and so is Paige Dutton, the woman he left behind. Can Sutter and Paige mend their broken hearts together?

#2294 HOW TO MARRY A PRINCESS
The Bravo Royales • by Christine Rimmer
Tycoon Noah Cordell has a thing for princesses—specifically, Alice Bravo-Calabretti. Noah is a man who knows what he wants, but can he finagle his way into this free-spirited beauty's heart?

#2295 THANKSGIVING DADDY
Conard County: The Next Generation • by Rachel Lee
Pilot Edie Clapton saves navy SEAL Seth Hardin's life—and they celebrate with a passionate encounter. Little does Edie know she has a bundle of joy on the way...and possibly the love of a lifetime.

#2296 HOLIDAY BY DESIGN
The Hunt for Cinderella • by Patricia Kay
Fashion designer Joanna Spinelli has nothing in common with straitlaced Marcus Barlow—until they go into business together. Can impetuous Joanna and inflexible Marcus meet in the middle—where passion might ignite?

#2297 THE BABY MADE AT CHRISTMAS
The Cherry Sisters • by Lilian Darcy
Lee Cherry is living the life in Aspen, Colorado. But when she finds herself pregnant from a fling with handsome Mac Wheeler, she panics. Mac follows her home, but little do they know what Love plans for them both....

#2298 THE NANNY'S CHRISTMAS WISH
by Ami Weaver
Maggie Thelan wants to find her long-lost nephew, while Josh Tanner is eager to raise his son in peace. When Maggie signs on, incognito, as Cody's nanny, no one expects sparks to fly, but a true family begins to form....

HSECNM1013

REQUEST YOUR FREE BOOKS!

2 FREE NOVELS PLUS 2 FREE GIFTS!

HARLEQUIN®

SPECIAL EDITION

Life, Love & Family

YES! Please send me 2 FREE Harlequin® Special Edition novels and my 2 FREE gifts (gifts are worth about $10). After receiving them, if I don't wish to receive any more books, I can return the shipping statement marked "cancel." If I don't cancel, I will receive 6 brand-new novels every month and be billed just $4.74 per book in the U.S. or $5.24 per book in Canada. That's a savings of at least 14% off the cover price! It's quite a bargain! Shipping and handling is just 50¢ per book in the U.S. and 75¢ per book in Canada.* I understand that accepting the 2 free books and gifts places me under no obligation to buy anything. I can always return a shipment and cancel at any time. Even if I never buy another book, the two free books and gifts are mine to keep forever.

235/335 HDN F45Y

Name _____ (PLEASE PRINT) _____

Address _____ Apt. # _____

City _____ State/Prov. _____ Zip/Postal Code _____

Signature (if under 18, a parent or guardian must sign)

Mail to the Harlequin® Reader Service:
IN U.S.A.: P.O. Box 1867, Buffalo, NY 14240-1867
IN CANADA: P.O. Box 609, Fort Erie, Ontario L2A 5X3

Want to try two free books from another line?
Call 1-800-873-8635 or visit www.ReaderService.com.

* Terms and prices subject to change without notice. Prices do not include applicable taxes. Sales tax applicable in N.Y. Canadian residents will be charged applicable taxes. Offer not valid in Quebec. This offer is limited to one order per household. Not valid for current subscribers to Harlequin Special Edition books. All orders subject to credit approval. Credit or debit balances in a customer's account(s) may be offset by any other outstanding balance owed by or to the customer. Please allow 4 to 6 weeks for delivery. Offer available while quantities last.

Your Privacy—The Harlequin® Reader Service is committed to protecting your privacy. Our Privacy Policy is available online at www.ReaderService.com or upon request from the Harlequin Reader Service.

We make a portion of our mailing list available to reputable third parties that offer products we believe may interest you. If you prefer that we not exchange your name with third parties, or if you wish to clarify or modify your communication preferences, please visit us at www.ReaderService.com/consumerschoice or write to us at Harlequin Reader Service Preference Service, P.O. Box 9062, Buffalo, NY 14269. Include your complete name and address.

HSE13R

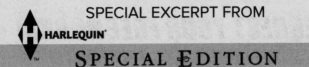
*Sutter Traub is a heartbreaker...something Paige Dalton
knows only too well. Which is why she's determined to
stay as far as she can from her ex! But Rust Creek's
prodigal son has come home to help his brother win
an election—and to win back the heart of the woman
he's never been able to forget...*

***

"Sutter?"

He yanked his gaze from her chest. "Yeah?"

She huffed out a breath and drew the lapels closer together.
Despite her apparent indignation, the flush in her cheeks and
the darkening of those chocolate-colored eyes proved that she
was feeling the same awareness that was heating his blood.

"I said there's beer and soda in the fridge, if you want a
drink while you're waiting."

"Sorry, I wasn't paying attention," he admitted. "I was thinking about how incredibly beautiful and desirable you are."

She pushed her sodden bangs away from her face. "I'm a
complete mess."

"Do you remember when we cut through the woods on the
way home from that party at Brooks Smith's house and you
slipped on the log bridge?"

She shuddered at the memory. "It wouldn't have been a big
deal if I'd fallen into water, but the recent drought had reduced

the stream to a trickle, and I ended up covered in muck and leaves."

And when they'd gotten back to the ranch, they'd stripped out of their muddy clothes and washed one another under the warm spray of the shower. Of course, the scrubbing away of dirt had soon turned into something else, and they'd made love until the water turned cold.

"Even then—covered in mud from head to toe—you were beautiful."

"You only said that because you wanted to get me naked."

"Just because I wanted to get you naked doesn't mean it wasn't true. And speaking of naked…"

"I should put some clothes on," Paige said.

"Don't go to any trouble on my account."

***

*We hope you enjoyed this sneak peek
from award-winning author Brenda Harlen's
new Harlequin® Special Edition book,
A MAVERICK UNDER THE MISTLETOE,
the next installment in*
MONTANA MAVERICKS: RUST CREEK COWBOYS.
Available next month.